Katherine Brankin

A SHOT FROM AFAR

Copyright ©2016 Kate (Katherine) Brankin.
All worldwide rights reserved. No part of this publication may be reproduced, stored in a retrieval system, or transmitted, in any form or by any means, electronic, mechanical, photocopying, recording or otherwise without the prior permission of Author.

First edition 2016
ISBN: 9780998428314

Published by DMD Books™
Deerfield, Illinois, USA

This is a work of fiction. Names, characters, places and incidents are either products of author's imagination or used fictitiously. Any resemblance to actual events or locations or persons, living or dead, is entirely coincidental. Any and all product names referenced within this book are the copyright and/ or trademarks of the respective owners. None of these owners sponsored, authorized, endorsed, or approved this book in any way. The author and publisher specifically disclaim all the responsibility for any liability, loss, or risk, personal or otherwise, which is incurred as a consequence, directly or indirectly in relation to this book.

A SHOT FROM AFAR

The Bennett Trilogy Book II

To my boys, always.

Acknowledgements

It's a lot harder to write a second novel than the first one. And it takes a lot more people to help you along the way. I would love to thank from the bottom of my heart a very special group of people. My favorite Sicilian Chef, and his Irish partner in crime—thank you for keeping me in truffle oil, hand-made salamis, and those delicious marinated olives, and for transporting me to Sicily with every amazing bite. To lovely and wonderful ER and the whole ACK Family—thank you for your support, your cheerleading, your advice on Italian style, all the chocolate, and black caviar and Veuve. To E3 and MC—there are not enough words to describe your wonderful support. To all my girls—thank you for being patient as my life suddenly got in the way of this release. To SS—thank you for agreeing to be my editor. To AA—fingers crossed!

Prologue

Karlovy Vary, Czech Republic

There was something strange, fake, about a couple over-enjoying their breakfast in the hotel's outdoor café. The woman—garishly dressed in designer garments and fur, two sizes too small, and dripping in jewels so early in the morning—kept taking duck-faced selfies, yet her companion frowned and swore in French as he leaned out of the way every single time she extended her arm. He was impatient, drumming his short fingers on the little marble table and checking his large gold watch. Across the tree-lined street, a tall thin female in large sunglasses jogged by. Her high long ponytail swayed from side to side with every stride. She slowed down and jogged in place, slightly turning her head to look around, then picked up her pace again.

The vulgar woman now moved on to snapping photos of her breakfast, then feverishly tapping the phone screen with her long and pointy nails. Her companion's finger-drumming picked up intensity, making his annoyance clear. An obviously American man, holding a folded newspaper, sat at the empty table next to them. He pulled a bright red pack of cigarettes out of his pant pocket and put it on the edge of his table. A waiter came over to take his order but the man nervously waved him off. The pony-tailed jogger reappeared across the street, only from the opposite direction. The American suddenly stood up and clumsily, yet purposely, knocked his cigarettes off the table. The finger-drumming man immediately dove down to pick them up and hit the American's leg with his head. But instead of returning the pack, he slipped it inside his own coat. This was an exchange—awkward and badly executed. The American walked away in haste; the finger-drummer interrupted another selfie of his companion by yanking her up to her feet and dragging her inside the hotel, paying no attention to her loud protests.

The ponytailed jogger across the street, now kneeling down to retie a black running shoe, witnessed the entire scene. 'Hmm, no trade craft,' she thought as she returned to her jog. 'How strange…'

1

Paris, France

Christmas Day. The only day he was left alone. The children, laden with extravagant gifts, left in the early morning to return to their mother. The staff had the day off, and left the night before to join their loved ones. They would not be returning until tomorrow. Christmas was for families, so his usual hookers were not answering his calls. Even his bodyguards took off shortly after the children were loaded into the car. They set the alarm and made sure the path to the panic room was free and clear, before accepting their holiday bonuses and disappearing. The bodyguards would not be returning until tomorrow morning as well.

He poured himself a generous glass of Louis XIV cognac and plopped down on the white leather couch in the parlor with a sigh of relief. He took a long sip, closed his eyes and listened. Silence. The house was finally silent.

Silence was rare for him, in fact he feared it. He was never alone, always surrounded by his entourage. He felt safe with them, he viewed them all as a human shield. Except on Christmas. Every Christmas Day he was left all alone for 24 hours. He used that time to admire the contents of his safe, watch a porn flick or two, and drink himself into a stupor. His bodyguards would find him the next morning passed out on the floor of the panic room, usually still clutching his glass. This Christmas Day, he planned on a repeat performance.

He swallowed the rest of his cognac and shuffled in his fur-lined slippers through the all-white penthouse into the kitchen to see if the cook left him something to eat. On the way to the kitchen, he looked out the large windows over the Paris rooftops. The sky was gray and cloudy, he could barely make out the white shape of Basilique due Sacré-Coeur in the distance. He made his way into the kitchen, the only place he did not bother to remodel much. As he rummaged in the small fridge for some cheese, a strange feeling of being watched washed over him. He ignored it. He grabbed day-old croissants from a covered plate on the counter and slowly shuffled back out. A trail of crumbs followed him all the way into his bedroom.

He was sitting on the parquet floor in front of his open wall safe admiring his bearer bonds, sipping his Louis XIV, and licking the croissant crumbs off his fingers when—suddenly—his head was yanked back by the hair and something sharp sliced across his neck. Blood rushed out of the wound, he could not breathe. His hair was released and he crumpled to the floor. But he would take some time to die and his last moment would be agonizing. He lay on the floor, blood and air gurgling out of a huge ear-to-ear gash across his neck, watching his killer step over him and approach the open safe. The killer bent down, and he realized—to his horror—that the killer was a female. The same woman he tried, but failed, to pick up in Monte Carlo a couple of days before. She was dressed head-to-toe in white to blend into his all white interior. The woman gently rummaged through the contents of the safe with a gloved hand, more out of curiosity than an attempt at a robbery. Among various papers, a micro SD card encased in a small plastic bag slid out. She picked it up to take a closer look, then slowly turned her head toward him. The last thing he ever saw—before the life exited his body—was her icy steel-blue eyes. There was no expression in her gaze, no excitement for the kill, no hate for her victim. Nothing but chilling, penetrating coldness. She watched as the last air bubble gurgled out of his throat and his eyes glazed over. Then she stood up and looked around the room. Listening. Nothing, not a sound. She slowly twisted the plastic bag with the SD card between her fingers, intrigued by the tiny handwritten label *Chen*, written above a crossed out *Moscou*, then slightly shook her head in refusal and returned the bag back to the same spot she found it. She left the premises the same way she came in—through an old kitchen dumbwaiter, next to the refrigerator, that everyone forgot about and never bothered to secure.

She slipped out of the side door of the building and quickly walked toward Avenue Victoria. There were cars and people around, but not many. She kept walking and was about to cross Rue Saint-Martin when a black motorcycle suddenly appeared out of nowhere. It slowed down next to her and then stopped, just long enough for her to jump on the back. As soon as her hands touched the rider's waist the motorcycle revved up and disappeared down the street. As the whining sound of the motorcycle dissipated in the air, huge white snowflakes started to slowly fall from the gray sky and clump together on the ground. The City of Lights was about to have a white Christmas.

2

Provincia di Palermo, Sicily

Between Palermo and Bagheria, in Provincia di Palermo, between the mountains and the Tyrrhenian Sea, La Famiglia Benedetto staked their claim. They were spread out among coastal towns and country villages, depending on their legitimate professions and personal preferences. They were a quiet Famiglia, there was no need to flex their muscles or display force in front of the neighbors in order to gain respect. Respect was earned a long time ago, and each generation gained more and more of it simply because everyone knew who the Benedettos really were.

They were assassins. Simply put, a clan of finely tuned, extremely well trained killers.

Every member of the Family, if needed, could kill without leaving a trace. But not everyone in the Family earned their living that way. That privilege was left to the select few, most of them Don Carlo Benedetto's—the current Capofamiglia—children and grandchildren. Don Carlo had a knack for choosing the perfect candidate for the profession, and he usually chose them while they were still young. Traditionally they were all males. With one exception. That exception was Catalina Benedetto, or Bennett outside Sicily. Catalina was Franco Benedetto's younger daughter, Don Carlo's granddaughter.

Catalina preferred to live by the coast. Her spacious villa had panoramic views of the Tyrrhenian Sea and took every advantage from the cooling sea breeze. Large, mature citrus and olive trees filled the vast property, which over a year ago became surrounded by a high stone wall, complete with a state-of-the-art security system and around the clock armed guards. The over-the-top security made the property stand out from the neighbors, but no one really cared or paid attention. Everyone knew who the resident was anyway. And everyone kept their mouth shut because the last thing anyone wanted was for a member of La Famiglia Benedetto to pay them a quiet, but deadly, visit.

Don Carlo lived on the outskirts of Bagheria, in a large old estate originally built in neoclassical style sometime in the late 1700s. Bagheria "the land that descends toward the sea"—originally a favorite vacation spot of the Palermo elite—was a town of densely-packed old stone buildings with red tile rooftops, and blue and white fishing boats bobbing up and down in the clear blue waters of the Tyrrhenian Sea. Tourists came to look at the grotesque stone statues dotting the walls of the historic Baroque mansion Villa Palagonia and to feast on delicious cannoli from Antica Pasticceria Don Gino. A member of Don Carlo's staff stopped by there often for a huge platter of sweets for the family. Catalina loved the uneven streets of the town, crumbling stone walls, old men in caps standing in front of shops smoking and complaining, old widows in cotton house dresses haggling over the freshness of produce. Don Carlo's estate, even though sitting just outside of town, had the same old feel, the same smells.

The estate belonged to the Family and came with the post of Capofamiglia. For generations, every Capo had lived there. They all added on, redecorated, and made improvements to the estate—some were good and some bad. Don Carlo's contributions were a heli pad and a large, climate-controlled garage for his vast collection of super cars. However, the garage was never full because Don Carlo's children and grandchildren were encouraged to use the cars and half the collection was gone at any time. Most of the cars were usually present on the estate on Sundays, when the family—except the ones working—gathered for their traditional Sunday dinner.

Frank, Catalina's father, chose to live out in the country-side, up in the mountains. Six months ago after moving back to Sicily from the Caymans, he took over the Family's olive oil and wine interests. It did not take long for him to take on a persona of a grumpy farmer, complaining about the crops and the weather, and patrolling his fields with a .50 caliber rifle looking for any sign of trespassers: be that animal or human.

The joyful blue late-afternoon skies of Christmas Day were suddenly disturbed by the buzzing of a helicopter. The chopper made a turn over Bagheria and headed in the direction of the wealthy estates. Nonna Rosalia looked up from her usual perch on the ancient stone steps of her home just as the chopper whizzed by, squinted her wrin-kled face in concentration, and—after recognizing the noisy intruder—shook her head before banging on the massive wooden door behind her and yelling in Sicilian dialect down the hall to her young grandson: "Ferruc-cio, get back to Don Benedetto's house! And don't for-get the salami!" Young Ferruccio worked in Don Carlo's household, but was spending Christmas with his family in Nonna Rosalia's house. He was expected back at the estate in time for the Benedetto's Christmas Day dinner. The dinner was delayed due to the absence of Don Carlo's granddaughter, Catalina. The appearance of the helicopter finally signaled her arrival. Ferruccio popped out of the house, tightly squeezing a very large fat salami wrapped in brown paper, kissed his Nonna goodbye, and sprinted down the street. The large salami was a Christmas present to the Benedettos from Nonna Rosalia. The old woman was proud of Ferruccio's employment and always paid her respects.

By the time he flew down the long gravel path leading up to the large stone villa, the helicopter was already silent. Two large men, Ferruccio recognized them as members of Catalina's *decina*, were loading several black cases and a large flat wooden crate into the back of a brand new white Range Rover. They noticed Ferruccio and waved. Ferruccio waved back and continued his sprint into the villa. He did not want to be late for his duties.

The villa was large, old, and made of stone. It had somewhat faded blue shutters on the windows, and extremely tall and heavy wooden doors. Despite the large number of windows, the interior was cool and dark—the windows were covered in old and thick draperies. Tonight the whole house was lit up with an abundance of crystal chandeliers and scented Diptyque candles, and kept warm with roaring fires in its massive fireplaces. The floors were done in colorful ornate ceramic tiles, all handmade centuries ago and now carefully maintained by a handful of artisans. These floors were highly polished and very slippery, allowing Ferruccio to slide all the way down a long hallway from the front door straight into the kitchen in the back of the house. He slid through the doorway and halted right in middle.

After the dining room, the kitchen was the largest room in the villa. The kitchen was enlarged by the previous Don, and was a cavernous space with a vaulted ceiling and an enormous stone hearth on the back wall surrounded by large glass doors on either side that lead out to the garden. Wicker baskets of all shapes and sizes were hanging off the wood ceiling beams, along with dried bundles of herbs and large legs of curing meats. The floor was old terracotta tile, but the walls were recently painted white per Catalina's instructions. She took over the kitchen recently, organizing it and bringing in modern appliances. She installed commercial refrigerators, a whole row of dishwashers, large restaurant sinks, and two La Cornue ranges. Each range was six feet long in blue enamel with gleaming brass trim. Today, every inch of cooking surface was occupied by various pots and pans bubbling and sizzling away. The middle of the kitchen was dominated by a massive butcher block table, as old as the house. Right now it was the center of meal preparation, but Ferruccio knew that once the family was served, the butcher block table would be cleared, covered with a white linen cloth, and set for a feast for the household staff. Whatever was served to Don Carlo's family was also served to his staff. It was an old tradition that was started by Don Carlo's great-great-grandfather Don Luigi. Don Luigi had a deep fear of being poisoned, making his staff eat the same meal guaranteed that no one would poison his dinner since they would be killing themselves as well. This tradition was kept in their own homes by all the Benedettos.

Ferruccio guessed that it was going to be a fabulous feast by the irresistible smells emanating from every square inch of this space, as well as two large whole pigs roasting on a spit over an open fire in the hearth. His hunch was confirmed when he noticed Catalina by one of the stoves, tasting something from a large bubbling pot. Her presence in the kitchen meant that she was in charge of the menu. Catalina added something to the pot, then turned around and yelled out instructions to someone in the back of the kitchen. There was so much noise, Ferruccio could not make out what she said. Neither did he notice her coming over to him, until she was standing right in front of his nose.

"Ciao, Ferruccio!" she said calmly. He startled and dropped the salami. It rolled slowly a couple of feet and stopped by the carved leg of the massive butcher block table.

"Scusi!" shot out Ferruccio in apology and stumbled to pick up the salami. She squeezed his shoulder to stop him.

"Aaahh, Ferruccio, leave it, I got it. You're too jumpy, we'll have to work on that." She said to him in English soothingly. She always talked to him in English, so he could practice his language skills. Catalina bent over and picked up the large salami. She carefully unwrapped one end and took a deep whiff of the cured meat. She closed her eyes in pleasure, the salami was fragrant and perfect. As always. "Please thank your Nonna for me for this lovely salami. Your family always makes the best. Now, off you go! We're almost ready to eat!" And she waved him off. He nodded and ran out of the kitchen.

Ferruccio ran all the way upstairs to the little attic room he shared with one of Don Carlo's bodyguards. He thoroughly washed his hands and face and quickly changed into his uniform of a white shirt and black suit and tie, then rushed back downstairs in search of Don Carlo's butler to receive his instructions for the evening. The Benedetto family Christmas Day dinner was about to be served.

3

Christmas Day was one of the rare occasions when all of Don Carlo's children, along with their families, gathered together. That was not always the case. When Catalina's father Frank lived in the States with his family, he never bothered to come to Sicily for Christmas. Catalina made it a point to be present every year since she became a made member of the Family. Everyone was excited to see her, but she was treated as one of the men and was never bothered with conversations about family life and children. She was never upset about this; she was always more interested in discussing the latest explosives and the conversion rates of various currencies than diapers and tutors. Her brother Mark was absent from the family table this year. He was still in the States and was cautious about his overseas travel.

Don Carlo had nine children. Five males and four females: Nunzio, Enzo, Paolo, Franco, Alessandro, Stefania, Anna Maria, Simonetta, and Giovanna. Alessandro and Anna Maria followed a higher calling, Alessandro became a priest and Anna Maria joined a convent. Don Carlo sometimes joked that with two children in the church, he was guaranteed a place in Heaven. Alessandro lived in Milan and recently became a Monsignor. He spent an hour every morning praying for the safety of his family. Anna Maria lived a quiet life in Palermo, and was always ready to help any family member in need. When Catalina lost her mother, Anna Maria came to the States to help Franco out with the children. It was she whom Catalina turned to for advice when she decided to protect her father's honor and join the family business.

The seven remaining children all were married and had children and grandchildren of their own. The average number was two. Paolo had one—now a furniture designer in Milan, and Giovanna had four—all in the restaurant business with two younger ones running successful nightclubs in Palermo and London.

Catalina's Zio Nunzio was the oldest of the nine children. He was also the shortest in the family, and fat. He had a booming voice and a dry wit, and believed that any problem could be solved by a block of C4 proportionate in scale to the size of the problem. Nunzio was the family's explosive expert, a skill that he passed on to his two sons. These days he ran the Family's meat business—the pigs and the veal on the dinner table came from his farm. His youngest son decided early on to follow his dad into the meat business instead of running around the world blowing things up. He spent his time researching the latest breeding techniques, and occasionally helping his brother experiment with different explosives. Catalina mentally filed him under the 'brain' category. One day she realized that everyone in the Family could be divided into three categories: brain, muscle, waste. She had been slowly categorizing everyone ever since. She put herself into the 'muscle' category. But if Zio Nunzio would have his way, she would be in the 'brain' column—hoping that one day she would become 'The Brain' by succeeding Don Carlo as the Capo. His opinion was shared by the Consigliere to La Famiglia Benedetto, Luciano Benedetto. Luciano was Don Carlo's baby brother, but had no intention of succeeding his brother. He loved being the Consigliere. Luciano and his family were also always present at the Christmas Day dinner table.

Nunzio's wife, Nadia, was the complete opposite of her husband. She was tall and rail-thin with a large hawk-like nose. She was flashy and loud, and wore Versace almost exclusively. She had a lot of work done, but surprisingly never had her nose fixed. Nadia smoked all the time, constantly drank espressos, and had her teeth veneered so they would be sparkling white just so not to change any of the unhealthy habits. Catalina found her visually appalling, but still held her in high regard. It was Zio Nunzio and Zia Nadia who took in her younger brother Mark and his premature baby girl when he had to disappear from the States, and it was Zia Nadia who taught Mark how to be a parent and demanded that he finally wise up and join the Family. When Mark returned to the States he was the son and the brother Frank and Catalina always wanted. And loud-mouthed Zia Nadia was credited with the transformation.

Zio Enzo loved his fruit. He had a large farm that grew all the produce for the Family. His pride and joy were his orange trees, he even exported the fruit overseas to luxury hotels and restaurants at high premium. Once in a while he would still pull a job, he was a talented marksman and liked to stay on top of his game. Catalina still trained with him from time to time. Enzo hated dressing up—an old shirt and jeans were his standard uniform, no matter what the occasion. Enzo was married to a small rotund woman, and the two of them somehow managed to produce impeccably dressed children with super model looks who were allergic to citrus.

Zio Paolo was a builder. Tall, thin, tan, with gold rimmed glasses and a thin black mustache, he was quiet and stern yet warm toward the children. In his younger years, his unique skill was to make people disappear. When he was tasked with a job, his mark would simply vanish without a trace. He never revealed the location of where he stashed the bodies, even to the Family. Now, in his retirement, he enjoyed building. He built Catalina's villa, and just like his bodies, would take its secrets to his grave.

Stefania, Simonetta, and Giovanna were like three peas in a pod. They looked the same, talked the same: loudly and always about the children, and dressed the same: in Dolce&Gabbana head to toe. In black. Simonetta and Giovanna even vacationed together, to the dismay of Don Carlo. Catalina simply referred to them as The Triplets. Collectively, they were a force to be reckoned with—they always got what they wanted. All three women married wisely: they chose men whose talents would complement the Family's gene pool, love came later. Their husbands were quiet, obedient, and efficient men, who always knew when to put a lid on their wives' shenanigans.

The black lacquer dining room table was custom-made by Italian craftsmen who specialized in making furniture for castles. The table was generously sized to accommodate all the adults and was trimmed out in 24-carat gold leaf. The younger children were seated at a separate table set up in the great room. They were not old enough for adult table conversations, nor could they sit still for the entire meal, which could last several hours. The great room was equipped with a state-of-the-art entertainment system and every toy imaginable, the teenagers were tasked with keeping the little ones in line and in one place. There was an incentive to this arrangement, the longer the adult time went undisturbed the larger the wad of cash was for each teenager at the end of the night. In typical Benedetto fashion, the teens organized and ran the great room with a steel hand, letting their parents enjoy the time with each other all the way past dessert. This year Catalina made their task easier by gifting everyone the latest tech gadgets and fancy colorful headphones.

Even though the dining table was big enough for all, having an adequate amount of chairs was always a problem. Ferruccio was tasked by the butler to collect the chairs around the house and make sure they were sturdy enough to hold the Benedetto men. Ferruccio knew that every year Nunzio would always break the chair he was sitting on, crashing to the floor and erupting in thundering laughter. Ferruccio wondered if this was done on purpose, and decided to test his theory by providing an office chair for Nunzio to sit on. His wife was given a tiny folding chair after Ferruccio overheard Catalina remarking that Zia Nadia was so thin 'she could sit on a toothpick.' He took special care when choosing seating for Don Carlo and Catalina, an effort that did not go unnoticed.

Tonight, the table was set with fine china and Irish linen. Flowers, tall crystal candelabras, baskets of freshly-baked bread, and platters of antipasto filled the spaces between place settings. *Opulence and abundance* came to mind when looking at the table, and that was before all the food arrived. As soon as the last candle was lit, Don Carlo's butler stepped into the living room to announce that dinner was about to be served.

4

They talked and ate at the same time. Rolled pieces of mortadella and salami from antipasto platters were used to accentuate a point by shaking them in someone's face, and pieces of bread doubled as tiles to demonstrate a new pattern being laid out in someone's pool. Catalina, however, said little, ate a lot, and people-watched. Between courses, she would lean back in her chair with a glass of wine in her hand to observe her family and hone in on conversations. Don Carlo, who exhibited the same behavior, watched her with great interest.

Primo, the first course, was a serious matter to Sicilians. Primo followed the appetite-inducing antipasto and was designed to build anticipation for the main course. *Primi piatti* (first dish) differed between Sicily's nine provinces reflecting the local ingredients, and the Benedettos served the traditional Palermo *Pasta con le Sarde* (pasta with sardines). On Christmas, they also served *Pasta Fritta alla Siracusana* (fried vermicelli) from Siracusa because Zio Nunzio loved the crunchy texture and the honey and orange sauce that covered the pasta. It was a last minute addition to the menu—demanded by Nunzio—that Catalina chose not to argue over. A large bowl of *Pasta Fritta alla Siracusana* was brought into the dining room with great pomp and circumstance and placed directly in front of Nunzio and Nadia. The table went quiet for a moment over such presentation and Nunzio shot a look to Catalina. She simply raised her glass to him in a silent toast that spoke volumes, and smiled. Nadia burst out laughing at the exchange, before piling a huge heap of pasta onto Nunzio's plate. She knew that this was the last time her husband would demand anything from Catalina.

Secondo, the main course, followed about half an hour after. The large roasted pig was wheeled on a cart into the dining room and then plated individually to everyone. The men cheered when the pig appeared, with Nunzio loudly boasting that the animal came from his farm and that Don Carlo personally selected it. *Farsumagru* (stuffed veal roulade) made from Simonetta's recipe came next, along with *Il Timballo del Gattopadro* (macaroni pie) which was Frank's favorite. Out of respect to Zio Alessandro's position, Catalina also served marinated freshwater whitefish which was flown in fresh from Lake Como that morning.

Contorno, vegetable side dishes, were served at the same time as well. *Caponata* and *Insalata Caprese* were presented along with a light green salad in case someone was on a diet and wanted to lighten their fare.

Formaggio e frutta, cheese and fruit, finished off the meal. By this point in the evening Nunzio had already broken his chair by rocking back and forth, Simonetta and Giovanna planned another joint family vacation which would later be vetoed by Don Carlo, Paolo had fallen asleep in his seat from too much good food and wine, and Frank had disappeared into the quiet calm of the library. About ten minutes into *formaggio,* Don Carlo got up and announced that dinner was over and that dessert would be served in the drawing room. At this point Alessandro said his goodbyes and went to his guest room. The women, except Catalina, went off to check on the children. The men invaded Frank's peace in the library. Catalina followed the men. She was expected to.

Every Christmas the made men of La Famiglia Benedetto, the ones that chose the art of assassination as their profession, would gather in Don Carlo's office to silently toast staying alive yet another year. Alessandro was well aware of this tradition, it was the reason why he retired to his bedroom right after dinner—he prayed for the souls of his family as they toasted their survival downstairs. Catalina, being a made member of the Family, was part of this tradition. And after being almost blown up to bits in Miami, she took it very seriously.

Don Carlo sat down behind his desk; Nunzio claimed the blue velvet sofa and unbuttoned his shirt; Catalina gracefully folded herself into one of the tan leather Wassily chairs by the marble fireplace; the rest of the men stood around the room, some leaning on furniture and walls for post-dinner support. Cigars were passed around, but Catalina declined. She kicked off her cobalt blue and nude platform Louboutins and stretched out her long legs. Don Carlo watched her as he puffed away on his cigar—tonight Catalina wore an intricately embroidered pale taupe gown by Ermanno Scervino with long sleeves and high neck. Her long hair was pulled back into a loose knot. She accessorized with a Chanel diamond watch and Cartier earrings that Don Carlo gifted her for Christmas. When he asked her what she wanted these holidays, she struck a pose and pulled a line from a famous actress "Cartier, darling! Cartier!" He left a pile of red leather boxes in her guestroom last night. Her outfit tonight was a stark contrast to the rest of the women—there was no restraint in their choices even though they all wore haute couture. Don Carlo liked Catalina's style: classic, minimal, perfectly edited.

The butler came in carrying a tray of crystal shot glasses, placed it on Don Carlo's desk, and quickly left. Don Carlo nodded to Luciano, who produced a crystal decanter with grappa. It was very old—it belonged to Don Carlo's predecessor. The flavor was almost gone at this point, but the strong alcohol remained. It was not for the faint of heart. Luciano filled the glasses, and everyone came over to the desk. They raised the glasses in a silent toast together, nodded to each other acknowledging yet another year of survival, and tossed back the drink quickly. The grappa was so potent, it absorbed right in the throat. Some of them slammed the glasses on the table, Don Carlo tossed his into the fireplace. It shattered against the bricks, fueling the fire with alcohol for a moment. Catalina gently set down the glass on a tiny table next to her chair. The decanter disappeared back inside the safe, it only made an appearance once a year on Christmas.

Next, the ledgers came out. Don Carlo slid his glasses down to the tip of his nose and paged through the books with the aid of a pencil, periodically lifting his head and looking at various family members. This was just for show, he knew exactly how much everyone brought in and what their share was. When he closed the last ledger with a snap, Luciano circled the room handing out fat envelopes to everyone. The money was sort of a holiday bonus, Catalina would distribute hers among her crew. Frank and Nunzio would do the same, Enzo would stash his into the mattress, and Paolo would give his money to his son to be put into his furniture business.

Once all the official business was concluded, everyone relaxed. Nunzio started talking explosives with his sons and Paolo, Frank chatted with Enzo about crops, Catalina slid back down into her perch by the fireplace and silently watched everyone. So did Don Carlo. Luciano stood quietly off to the side of Don Carlo's desk, his usual place, and observed both Don Carlo and Catalina. 'She's next,' he thought.

5

The last bite of dessert eaten, the last drop of espresso drank, the last of the relatives driven off, Don Carlo and Catalina were finally alone. Frank left early, right after the toast, Anna Maria snuck out when the dessert arrived, Nunzio was the last to leave. Catalina finally kissed him goodnight and forced him out the door. Ferruccio had to help him to the car, he was too drunk to make it on his own. Catalina and Nonno adjourned to the loggia and sat without talking, looking at the Sicilian starry sky. The butler showed up with blankets, asking if there was anything else they required. Nonno asked for some sparkling water and Catalina indicated to an inch of something with her fingers and little wink. The butler knew instantly what she wanted—limoncello.

He returned with a bottle of San Pellegrino, two glasses, a cordial of limoncello, and a large plate of steamed octopus. Steamed octopus was always served at the end of the meal—when everything was cleared and the food was starting to digest—the simply prepared octopus with just a tiny squeeze of fresh lemon juice always hit the spot. Catalina held serving the octopus until everyone left, it was Nonno's favorite dish and she wanted him to enjoy it without having to fight everyone else for it. Nonno smiled when the saw the plate, he knew it was her doing.

"How was the Frenchman?" he asked before popping a deep purple curly tentacle into his mouth.

"Super short. And obnoxious. He had these unpleasant deep-set tiny beady eyes. And he bragged about his sexual escapades, in graphic detail, to any man that happened to be taller than him. So pretty much to everyone. The job took longer than needed, I had to chase him across half the continent. It would have been a lot easier as a long range job when he was hanging out in Karlovy Vary, and I wouldn't have to miss Christmas," Catalina answered before taking a slow sip of her limoncello. The limoncello had a rich bright yellow color and a smooth finish. Even though everyone made their own, Enzo produced the best and would send huge glass jugs of it to Nonno's house on a regular basis. Catalina eyed the octopus, but was not going to take any unless Nonno offered. He gestured to the plate and she took a piece.

"Well, the client was very specific and paid accordingly. We do what is asked… And it looks like we did a world a favor for taking care of him," he replied. "Found anything interesting, or did you not look around?"

"Well, his mistress was a lot taller than him, wore too much makeup, and was not a natural blond," Catalina said with a small smile. "I did find something—a micro SD card from a phone or a camera, which was strange since it was known that he refused to deal in tech. I left it where I found it though, no need to repeat history," she was referring to the research she took from a certain Dr. Wilson that painted a CIA target on her back a year and a half ago.

"Smart move, always learn from your mistakes," said Nonno picking up another octopus. "I see you brought home more hardware, are you stocking up?"

"Something like that. I don't want to be running to Eddie every five minutes."

"You could use others, he's not the only game in town," suggested Nonno. Catalina shook her head.

"No. Not yet. He's good for now," she said, yet Nonno could sense that there was a tiny seed of doubt about Eddie already. Ever since Frank suddenly abandoned his Cayman Islands estate and moved back to Sicily, Catalina started stocking up on ordinance. Eddie Washington, Catalina's friend and arms dealer, inadvertently bought the estate next to Frank's and quickly managed to annoy him. Frank mentioned that Eddie was living large, a remark that was not sitting well with Catalina.

They ate quietly for a while, looking up at the stars. There was a faint sound from the crashing waves in the distance. With everyone gone and the house finally silent, they were able to enjoy the calming hum of the Tyrrhenian Sea. Catalina stopped eating and was just staring into space. Nonno leaned back in his seat and watched her.

"You don't know him that well to miss him," he broke the silence. She did not turn her head.

"I can't help it. He crawled under my skin, I guess," she said quietly.

"It's unfinished business, that's what it is. You let him live when you shouldn't have and now it festers like a tumor. And Marco's doing whatever it is he's doing in New York does not help you, only makes this… this tumor… bigger. You need to move on, find someone else," advised Nonno. Catalina did not respond, her breathing as rhythmic as the distant crashing waves.

"I'm going to bed," suddenly said Nonno and stood up. Catalina got up as well, she was not staying. Nonno walked her to the front door, and tossed her the keys to his 1960 Alfa Romeo Giulietta SZ—it was going to be her ride for the night. They embraced to bid good night and Catalina got into the car. The engine roared to life, bringing out a smile in both Nonno and Catalina. Nonno tapped on the window right before she was about to pull away, she rolled it down.

"Let him go," Nonno said slowly. "Or finish him."

Catalina bit her lip in response, then shifted gears and sped off. Nonno shook his head and walked back inside.

The clothes came off one at a time, landing on the heated terrazzo floor in little heaps, leaving a tell-tale trail as she walked through the house. The shoes were the last to come off—in the bedroom. She turned on the stereo and Leonard Cohen's low voice came on as she lowered herself into the bubbling water in the enormous tub, drawn for her just before she arrived by her butler Fernando. She slid into the water up to her neck and gently floated, staring out of the large window by the tub. Her brain was busy processing the bits and pieces of information from conversations she overheard during dinner. Like the fact that Nunzio's son was about to set off an explosion big enough to make the news; that another citrus harvest was about to begin, which meant that tomorrow she'll have to order Antonia to get the farming crew ready; her father was finally happy with the winery operations; her cousin was thinking of having another baby, even though she already had five children; and the fact that the young Ferruccio did not miss a thing during the entire night. Catalina decided to test him soon to see if there was any potential in him for things other than serving dinner. She was wondering what her brother Mark and her little niece Sofia were up to in Brooklyn at this time, when images of her time with Agent Campbell suddenly awoke in her head. Again. Her face frowned and she closed her eyes. She lay still in the tub for a moment, before her hand felt around the edge for the stereo remote, her fingers finally finding the volume button. She turned up the music all the way, took a deep breath and completely submerged under water.

On the small patio outside the kitchen, Antonia and Fernando—Catalina's housekeeper and her personal butler—were passing the time with a quiet poker game.

They paused their game when the master bathroom lights went on indicating that their mistress was home, and they paused again when Cohen's voice suddenly filled the house. Fernando looked at Antonia with a question in his eyes, but she just shook her head, answering "It is better not to know" in Sicilian. Antonia was not about to explain that the reason every time loud music suddenly filled the house was because Catalina was attempting to suppress thoughts about a certain CIA Agent. An Agent she should have finished off in Miami.

6

The high-pitched whining of a drill, followed by vibrating thuds of a hammer slamming on metal, suddenly pounded into Catalina's head, rudely waking her up. She sat up in her bed, shook her head gently to clear her mind, and tried to figure out where all the racket was coming from. The pool.

Catalina marched to the wall of windows and ripped open the curtains. Bright morning sun reflecting off the pool water hit her eyes and she squinted to adjust. She saw large boxes and men with tools everywhere, and in the middle of all the noise and chaos was her father barking orders in rapid Sicilian and gesturing with his coffee cup. She groaned and slid open the large glass panel.

"What on earth are you doing?" she yelled out. The men turned toward her, then quickly averted their gaze—she was wearing a very small lace nightgown. Frank gestured more orders with his coffee cup and came over.

"You have all this patio furniture sitting in Paolo's truck for months now, so I decided to help you unpack it," said Frank, walking into her bedroom and closing the curtains behind him.

"I was rather busy as you know!" Catalina snapped and crossed her arms. She narrowed her eyes slightly in disapproval of Frank's intrusion.

"I see… La Perla?" he shot back, nodding to her lace nightie with his chin.

"Yes, La Perla!" Catalina turned and headed toward the bathroom.

"You really should cover up in front of your men, *cara mia!*" pointed out Frank.

"My men don't make it a habit of disturbing my sleep," she reported. "Why are you really here?"

"Breakfast!" answered Frank, then turned and walked back out to the pool. Catalina slammed her bathroom door in response.

Frank came to breakfast often. They would discuss Mark and his daughter Sofia, Mark communicated mostly with Frank and on a rare occasion he would call Catalina on a burner phone. Those calls where brief and far between, Mark was being extremely cautious. Frank knew more of the details of Mark's daily life, and he would share them with Catalina over morning cappuccinos and fruit. Catalina sometimes would tell him an interesting tidbit from her recent job travel, but never gave out any work details. Today was no exception.

"So here's a story," started Catalina after a tray laden with brioche, freshly squeezed juice from blood oranges, and cappuccinos was brought to them in the dining room. Catalina preferred to take her breakfast outside on the covered loggia, but today the loggia and the patio surrounding the pool were overtaken by the new outdoor furniture that was being unpacked and assembled by Catalina's men. She was still sore over Frank's intrusion into her private business, but decided to let it go. For now.

"I was on my way back from scouting exit points in Paris, I was starving, and suddenly I see this tiny little restaurant in Île de la Cité. It was just a big wooden old door, and a menu on the window. Looked charming, smelled delicious, so I went inside. It's a super narrow and long space, and dark toward the back—actually quite convenient for us," she said with a wink. "There is no room for the kitchen, it's in the basement and they have to bring the food up by a dumbwaiter. I get seated in the back, at this tiny table. The place is so small, there only enough room to squeeze sideways between the tables and you better be thin. There are two couples, Brits, next to me. Well, one was talking about going back to Belfast, but still… Brits. Starched shirt collars, wool sweaters, women in pearls. You know the type—uptight cocks," Frank nodded in understanding, Catalina reached for the brioche and continued.

"The waiter comes over, we chat just a bit, I put in my order, he's very polite. Then he turns to the Brits and they rip him a new one about their food being late and that they're going to miss their train back to London. They came to Paris for lunch, apparently. He tells them that they can't cancel their order because it was already being prepared and storms off. He returns shortly with the plates and throws them down at their table, the plates even rattled around for a while before settling," she made a swirling gesture with her finger, demonstrating the rattling of the plates on the table. "Then he slowly turns to me, and in a sweet and extremely polite tone asks if I would like some wine." Frank leaned back in his chair and let out a laugh. He could just imagine how much control Catalina had to muster not to finish those idiots off. He would have had hard time controlling himself.

"Aah, those French waiters, don't mess with them! I bet he spat into their food as well!" chuckled Frank.

"Wouldn't put it past him!" replied Catalina. "That dumbwaiter they used though… was quite inspirational…" Frank did not inquire, he knew the comment was related to her job.

They moved on to talking about Mark, he called on Christmas day and told Frank about being set up by his well-meaning landlords on yet another blind date. Mark could not understand why they kept setting him up, but Frank knew that Catalina asked the old couple to find Mark a good Jewish girl. Of course he kept that information to himself, he immensely enjoyed Mark's suffering.

Their conversation was interrupted from time to time by the ruckus coming from the outside. Catalina would frown every time and rip apart her brioche, but Frank just smiled. They were almost done with breakfast when Fernando appeared.

"Mi Scusi!" said the butler. He put a cell phone in front of Catalina and left. Catalina glanced at the phone, she had an encrypted message. She swiped right and punched a code to decrypt. The message simply said <Berlin.> She had another contract. Catalina tossed her napkin on the table and got up. Breakfast was over.

7

Berlin, Germany

Herr Hermann's real name was Gonzales. He was a crook and a liar who came to Europe from the States about a decade ago and conned and stole his way from one wealthy European woman to the next. He had a price on his head for years now, but changed his identity and looks so many times that he was almost impossible to track down. Until the Benedettos got involved. They quickly honed in on his stench and tracked him to Berlin.

The large metal suitcase he just stole was heavy and he struggled with it all the way from the parking garage elevator to his black BMW 5-series sedan. He had no clue what was in it, he did not get a chance to check out the contents yet. It was strangely cool to the touch—a bit damp on the bottom—but he was not smart enough to consider that maybe he should pass on this one.

The parking level was dark and quiet. He looked around, but did not see anyone. He continued to struggle with the suitcase until he finally reached his car. Gonzales fumbled with the key fob trying to release the trunk, when:

"Yo! Gonzales!" a female voice called out. He turned around and saw a tall blonde emerge from behind a parked SUV. He did not recognize her, but the hair style—the same wispy, bouncy, medium length blond—reminded him of the woman he recently conned. The woman started walking toward him, the clicking of her stilettos echoing throughout the parking level. She was carrying a dark coat in her arms.

"You're a hard man to track, you know that?" she said loudly in a strong American accent. But before he could respond, she put two bullets into his torso. The gun made just two fast soft clap sounds, and the coat hid the muzzle flash. The shots were not meant to kill instantly, but do enough damage for Gonzales to bleed to death. Slowly.

Gonzales collapsed onto the ground, his key fob falling just out of his reach. The blonde walked over and stepped on his hand, purposely, as she bent down to pick up the key fob. She shifted her weight and slowly turned her foot, crushing his hand even further as she popped the trunk of the BMW. The trunk was completely lined with plastic—something that was not there, nor did Gonzales do when he parked the car an hour ago. She tossed aside her coat, holstered her gun under her jacket, then heaved Gonzales off the ground by his armpits and shoved him into the trunk. He groaned in pain and feebly attempted to resist. She simply shoved him deeper into the plastic-lined trunk.

Once he was completely inside, she paused—listening for anything that would interrupt her. Quiet. She continued by knocking over the suitcase with her high-heeled foot. Gonzales was still conscious enough to hear the heavy thud of the suitcase and the locks being popped open. She either knew the lock combination, or had a key. What he heard next sounded like crunching and suddenly something heavy, hard, wet, and incredibly cold landed next to him. A bag of ice. The suitcase contained bags of ice. And she was packing him in with the bags. The last bag ripped open when she picked it up, so she simply poured the ice cubes on top of him before slamming the trunk shut. Some ice cubes fell on the ground and she kicked them out of the way before putting her coat inside the suitcase and tossing it onto the back seat of the BMW. She got into the car and pulled out.

By the time the car reached the exit gate, the blonde had on large highly-reflective aviator shades. She stopped in front of the attendant, but instead of handing him her parking slip, she gave him a thick envelope. The parking attendant watched the car disappear down the street, chuckling a little at a red bumper sticker that said in German 'Mutti is watching you,' before reaching under his chair for a large bottle of bleach and some rubber gloves. He left his post and quickly proceeded to the level where the BMW sedan was parked just moments ago.

8

New York, USA

The fallout from the failed attempt of the CIA's wet team, headed by Special Agent in Charge Jim Campbell, to hunt down Catalina Bennett in Miami was huge. First there was an issue of the CIA operating within United States—which was illegal. The Agency body count was also not in Agent Campbell's favor as well: five dead, Campbell himself was heavily wounded. Two Miami highrises were damaged, the handiwork of only one person, the one highrise happened to be a very expensive hotel. The high-speed boat chase, which ended in a fiery explosion, drew the attention of national news. No remains were recovered from the boat explosion. When the fire finally died, all that was found in the melted heap of plastic were the remains of weapons and bullets.

Both Campbell and his probie agent Nick McCarthy were debriefed for weeks. In the end, the case files for Operation Darwin were heavily redacted and sealed. Catalina was declared dead by the CIA and, after a long analysis, it was decided that the Benedetto mafia family posed no real threat. This however did not sit well with McCarthy, who was convinced that the Benedettos were becoming more dangerous by the minute and were responsible for almost all high profile assassinations. He was told to mind his own business, which made him even more obsessed with the Family. But after a while he seemed to calm down and moved on with other projects. Campbell had no idea that McCarthy continued his digging into the Benedettos off the clock, quietly, at home.

Eventually life in the New York office of Special Activities Division went back to normal. And then, exactly six months to the date of Catalina's death in Miami, all hell broke loose. The Benedettos, the 'small Sicilian mafia family that posed no threat to the Agency,' retaliated for the death of one of their own. In a typical mafia fashion, they assassinated almost everyone that was involved with Operation Darwin. Dr. Wilson's widow; her father, who was the one to hire Catalina to kill Dr. Wilson in the name of his daughter's honor; and the MI6 agent, a friend of the father's, the one that recommended Catalina for the job. All three were killed at almost the same time, close range with two shots. And just for good measure, in case the Company did not get the message, the head of the Italian desk was also picked off in the same manner right before he was about to walk into his office in Rome. The final 'nail in the coffin' as McCarthy called it, was when McCarthy and Campbell's US safe houses were ransacked. However, their primary residences were left untouched. And, for some reason, their lives were spared as well. McCarthy was convinced that it was not over, that their deaths were simply postponed. The Benedettos moved up to the persons-of-interest list, but no one was willing to go after them. The Company bowed its head in defeat and retreated. For now.

9

New York, CIA office, Special Activities Division

"Luxury vessel blows up off the coast of Monaco."

"Ten board members of Primrose Corporation killed in massive explosion."

"Primrose Corp. is refusing to comment on deaths of its board members as founder's son takes control of the company. Stock doubled."

McCarthy was reading out loud the headlines as he dropped each newspaper on Campbell's desk. Campbell waited for him to be finished then scooped up the papers and dropped them into the trash.

"Not our gig, I told you! Leave this one alone!" Campbell barked. McCarthy was bugging him ever since the Monaco desk reported the explosion of an extremely expensive mega-yacht in Monaco's waters, including an interesting note that there was no prior chatter about it and no one was taking credit. McCarthy was convinced it was another Benedetto job, yet Campbell shut down all his inquiries. McCarthy leaned over and rummaged through the garbage can. "What are you doing?" demanded Campbell.

"Peel needs the French one, he ordered all the French papers brought to his office," answered McCarthy.

"Now that *is* of interest," said Campbell quietly. "He's been combing through the French news for days. Yet he did not assign anything to anyone. I wonder what it is he's looking for. Keep an eye on it, will you? But quietly, or we'll end up in the basement."

McCarthy nodded in response, folded up the French paper he fished out of Campbell's trash, and started to walk slowly toward Peel's glass office.

William Peel III was now overseeing, among his other numerous somewhat shady duties, all of Campbell's operations. After the big fiasco in Miami, where he lost his team and was blamed for the large and bloody hole in the Epic hotel, Campbell now had to take orders from a career pencil pusher with no field experience. Peel got into the CIA through family connections, then backstabbed and blackmailed his way up the ladder with hope that the CIA gig would lead to a lucrative job in the private sector with a high six figure salary. He reasoned that if it worked for his father, it should work for him. Yet, with no real coveted skills, besides brilliant dirty politics, no one in the private sector wanted him. And so he bitterly stayed in the CIA, climbing the ladder, and taking on any shady and unethical operation that he came across. Soon the word spread around the Company that if you needed something nasty done yet wanted to still be able to sleep at night—give it Peel, nothing ever bothered him.

Campbell, along with McCarthy in tow, landed on Peel's team after Miami. It was a punishment: Campbell was no longer the Agent in Charge, he had to run every operational detail through Peel now. Most of his ideas where shut down, and for the ones that were approved, Peel took all the credit. Campbell knew exactly what was going on: he was being shut out, he was going to stay under Peel's thumb for the remainder of his career. Unless he retired, something he was not willing to do. Even though McCarthy begged him on an almost daily basis. McCarthy himself wanted to leave the Company and use private resources to track down the Benedetto Family. But Campbell was not retiring and McCarthy did not want to leave behind his friend and mentor alone in now hostile environment.

McCarthy found Peel sitting behind his massive white and chrome desk in his red, white and blue office. Peel spent his own money and brought in a decorator, yet the décor was obnoxious. The walls were upholstered in red and blue suede square panels, a white Alpaca hide rug covered the floor to hide the Company-installed gray carpet. He brought in modern art from his parents' summer home—large works by Andy Warhol and Keith Haring hung on the walls, an inflatable bunny by Jeff Koons sat on the desk. Campbell was dying to put a pin to it, yet restrained himself daily. There were two metal wire rod chairs, minus the cushion, in front of Peel's desk for visitors. No one wanted to sit down, everyone just hovered by the door, escaping at the first opportunity. No food or drink were allowed in the office, even though everyone knew that Peel kept booze in the bottom drawer of his desk. McCarthy missed Campbell's office, with its stale smell of Chinese food and Earl Grey tea and the constantly boiling old electric teakettle.

Peel was engrossed in some activity on his cell phone, McCarthy put the French newspaper in front of him without saying a word. Peel waved him off then watched him leave the office before sending the last text, to his bookie, and picking up the paper. He thoroughly looked through every headline, yet not finding what he was looking. Until suddenly, on the bottom of the last news page, there was a small mention that there were no new leads in the murder case of a body found in a Paris penthouse. The article went on to repeat previously reported details that the victim was discovered by his own bodyguards returning to work after a day off on Christmas, there was no trace of the killer, and that Interpol was looking into the case. At the end it mentioned that the victim's safe was left open. "Shit!" spat Peel, and crumbled the paper in anger. He then composed himself and looked out through his glass office walls at the cubicle floor to see if anyone noticed his outburst. No one seemed to be looking his way. He stuffed the paper into his briefcase and went back to work. Only he missed McCarthy standing behind the watercooler and pretending to be checking something on his phone. Peel did not realize that McCarthy was actually recording him reading the paper, and his outburst, with the phone.

Two weeks later

"Peel! I've got a potential distressed asset! Says she's blown!" Campbell burst into Peel's office. He stopped by the door, anxiously waiting for instructions.

"Who?" demanded Peel, leaning slightly forward in his chair.

"*Springhare*, she's a NOC. Penetration inside the Ukrainian government," said Campbell. Inside, he was slowly steaming, he felt that all these questions were wasting precious moments. Peel took his time before rendering his decision.

"Get her out," he ordered. Campbell threw his hands up in the air in a 'I could've told you that!' and rushed out the door to put the extraction plan in play.

Peel slumped into his chair, then slowly turned away from the glass wall. He did not want anyone to see panic on his face. He could hear orders being issued on the floor, phones ringing, people running around. 'And so it begins...' he said to himself in horror.

10

Provincia di Palermo, Sicily

Don Carlo Benedetto was 84 years old. He was tall, tan, still muscular, with short gray hair, a closely trimmed beard, and wore tortoise rimmed tinted glasses. Whether he actually needed the glasses or he wore them just to appear older and frailer to his enemies, no one really knew. Unlike Frank's and Catalina's cold steel-blue eyes, Don Carlo's eyes were warm brown. And capable of showing emotion, at least now at his old age. Mark, Catalina's brother looked exactly like him. He spoke slowly, with carefully chosen words. When Don Carlo took over La Famiglia Benedetto he was in his mid-forties. He took over after his uncle died from a ripe old age—an unusual way to go for a Benedetto. Don Carlo's own father died when Carlo was still very young during a contract job that went wrong—a normal way to die in this family.

Don Carlo's right to become the head of the family of killers was well earned. Carlo was extremely intelligent; lethal with a knife, his weapon of choice; and, thanks in part to his love of chess, a brilliant long-term strategist. He always kept a watchful eye on the Family business, even when he cut back on the killing to race Ferraris on the international circuit and chase after women.

His womanizing produced many children—he acknowledged all of them, supported all of them, and initiated the males into the Family once he became Capo. He never married. Until Catalina became a permanent fixture in his life, the only women around his house were the widows in the kitchen.

All the children in the Family were trained to kill from their young age, and the men were turned into lethal and effective killing machines. The women were expected to marry men that would either add to the talent pool or bring other revenue streams into the Family. Some married killers, some married craftsmen, farmers, and merchants. Over the years, the Family became self-sustaining: it produced its own food, procured the goods it needed through its own merchants, built its own villas. Don Carlo did not want to depend on anyone else but his own Famiglia. It was a closed loop, it allowed the Benedettos to be secure and stay neutral during any Mafia wars.

Under Don Carlo, the Family prospered and earned great respect from other Sicilian clans. Even the funerals were not happening as often as previously, Don Carlo making sure that every contract the Family took was planned to a minute detail taking into account all possibilities and always having several points of exit. His rein was proceeding smoothly, until one of his sons—Franco—decided to move to America against Don Carlo's wishes. Don Carlo blamed his daughter-in-law, a head-strong intelligent and educated beauty, who filled his son's head with ideas of independence and greener pastures across the pond. Franco promised to send the Family a share of his earnings and that his children would spend every summer in Sicily, but other than that the Family was asked to stay out of his life. Don Carlo pondered the matter over a silent game of chess with himself one night and reluctantly agreed. Franco moved to the US and became Frank Bennett. He continued his vocation as an assassin and made a pretty good living that way. Don Carlo silently watched from afar, accepted the Family's share from every job and never vocalized his disapproval when a certain handler appeared in Frank's life with pockets full of CIA contracts and cash. Don Carlo decided that it were Franco's children, son Marco and daughter Catalina, he should be working on bringing back into the Family fold. The kids came to stay with him every summer, arriving the day after school ended and leaving the day before it began. Don Carlo first concentrated his efforts on Marco, but it was Catalina that showed the most interest and always wanted to tag along. She would spend her mornings following her brother and Nonno, as Don Carlo was called by his grandchildren; her afternoons cooking with the women; and her evenings joining Marco and Nonno in a game of chess. On really scorching Sicilian summer days she would find refuge from the heat in Nonno's dark and cool library, losing herself for hours in his vast collection of art books.

Marco spent increasingly more time tinkering with computers and electronics, and avoiding Nonno's target practices at all costs. Catalina, on the other hand, showed remarkable talent and one summer announced matter-of-factly that she was fully aware of the Family business and wanted to be a part of it one day. Nonno happily agreed. However, that day came a lot sooner than Nonno had planned—she was still in high school when she made her bones.

One morning, shortly after New Year's Day, Don Carlo woke up with a revelation that he hated his villa. He jumped out of bed and bellowed on top of his lungs for his butler, Inch. Moments later, the Benedetto Family Consigliere, Luciano Benedetto, was rustled out of his bed by a telephone call. He was informed by Inch that he was to find the best decorator on the island and bring him to Don Carlo's villa immediately.

By lunch, the located decorator was trying to keep up after Don Carlo, who was rushing from room to room while barking his instructions and articulating everything with his hands. Don Carlo wanted a light and fresh space, something that would make him feel young again. And he wanted it right now. This being Sicily, they finally settled on four weeks from now, and Don Carlo and everyone else would have to move out while the work was being done. Don Carlo raised his eyebrow and said, in a calm voice and with no gestures, that his staff would stay put to keep an eye on the progress and that his son Paolo and Paolo's men would be doing the actual work. The decorator, who was sweating profusely at this point because he knew exactly who his new client was, wiped the sweat off his forehead with his linen handkerchief and nodded in approval. Don Carlo nodded back and finally waved the decorator off in dismissal. He then snapped his fingers to Inch, and by dinnertime Don Carlo was all settled in the guest quarters on his beloved granddaughter Catalina's estate. Two days later, she fled to the Caymans with all of her crew in tow.

11

The Cayman Islands

Seline and Eddie Washington were the only two people outside the Family that Catalina would call 'friends.' Eddie was her childhood friend as well as a very successful arms dealer. Seline was Eddie's wife. Catalina had a hand in getting them together. Even though Eddie and Catalina were close, they treaded with caution around each other. The truth was that Catalina scared Eddie to death. Unless she was shopping, he always made it a point to keep his merchandize as far away from her as possible. His only consolation was a theory that due to his enormous build, she would not be able to kill him with her bare hands. A theory he hoped he would never have to put to the test.

A year and a half ago, about the same time Catalina was wreaking havoc in Miami, Eddie made the move from Chicago to the Cayman Islands. He now owned a large villa on Grand Cayman. The villa was situated on a large plot of land along miles of private beach. There were a pool, a spa, a tennis court, a small putting green, a basketball court, and a large kid playground. Eddie had a dock and a small marina extending far enough into the water to house his yacht, a couple of go-fast boats, and an occasional seaplane.

The interior of the villa was decorated in white marble, modern wicker furniture, large leaf tropical plants, brass hardware, and navy and white stripes. There was an animal print once in a while, and sparkly crystal. High-end technology was everywhere, with enormous TVs in every room and game controllers littering the coffee tables.

"There is activity next door," reported Eddie's personal bodyguard Diamond, busting in on the family breakfast one morning.

"What kind of activity?" Eddie inquired with his mouth full of eggs.

"Looks like someone's moved in but I can't tell who."

"It's a Bennett estate, only one of them can move in there," calmly commented Seline. "You have nothing to worry about."

"Nothing to worry about… I still want to know which Bennett is it," countered Eddie and gave Seline a look. Diamond pretended not to notice. "Take a man or two and go snoop things out," ordered Eddie. "Quietly."

"And if we get caught? Claim *parlay* and hope they stick to the code?"

"Something like that!" Eddie said with a chuckle. His kids giggled. For the past several months, the kids got really into *The Pirates of the Caribbean*, watching one of the movies every night and playing pirates all day long. Pretty soon the entire household and Eddie's staff started quoting lines from the movies. The line "You smell funny!" was everyone's favorite—not surprising, due to the tropical heat and the fact that everyone was still getting used to it.

There were three of them—Catalina only recognized one from the vivid description her housekeeper gave her a while back. She could track them on the CCTV the moment they clumsily scaled over the stone wall surrounding her Cayman property. Catalina wondered whether or not she should give them the satisfaction of getting further into the property before announcing that the game was up. She watched with amusement as the three men attempted to quietly make a path from palm tree to palm tree—yet fail miserably. Her small crew gathered around her, watching the spectacle and trying extremely hard not to burst out in laughter in her presence. She looked at her men, and made a small gesture of amusement with her hand toward the CCTV screens. Unable to contain themselves any longer, the men broke out in laughter. She joined them with a small chuckle.

"Come on, time to pick them up," she finally said in Italian and headed outside. Her men drew their weapons and followed.

Diamond was about to leave his position behind a short but fat palm tree, when a little green dot suddenly appeared in the middle of his chest. He froze in fear—laser sight. He slowly, cautiously, dared to look up without moving his head. He discovered they were surrounded by a group of heavily armed men with semiautomatics. And then he heard clapping.

A tall, slender woman appeared from behind the armed men clapping slowly. She had dark flowing hair, long well-tanned legs clad in tiny white lace shorts, and wore a Kevlar vest over a loose silk tank top. She stopped a couple of feet in front of Diamond, and drew her gun from behind her back. Diamond dropped his own weapon and raised his hands in surrender. His two companions followed. She waved with her gun for them to come out of the palm trees. They complied.

"Diamond, I presume?" asked Catalina. Diamond silently nodded. "Let's get out of the sun, shall we?" she said and lowered her weapon. Her men, on the other hand, kept their weapons drawn. She motioned for Diamond to follow her and turned toward the house. He cautiously followed, hands still in the air.

Until today, Catalina never met Diamond. She was given a detailed description of the man—tall, dark, with super white flashy smile and a tight ass—by her housekeeper, Antonia. She also knew from Eddie that Diamond, following Eddie's orders, killed two men and blew up her DC townhouse to protect her identity. For that Diamond was handsomely rewarded by the Family in a form of a suitcase full of cash. Diamond, working for Eddie as his top bodyguard, felt weird about taking the money and promptly informed his boss about it. Eddie listened, then told him to take the money, since what he did was really not in his job description. 'Think of it as a bonus, and keep your mouth shut,' were the words Eddie used. Diamond stuffed the cash into a hole he made in his mattress, and prayed every night he would not have to encounter anyone from the Family again. Diamond was afraid of nothing but the Benedettos.

He followed Catalina into the house, waiting with every step for her to suddenly turn around and shoot him. After all, they trespassed on her property. But instead, she led them into a vast and spacious living room decorated in light muted tones and modern lines. The furniture had low clean lines, the deep sofas and chairs were upholstered in cool linen. There was not a toss pillow in sight. Catalina kicked off her Louboutin studded gladiator sandals, motioned for the three men to sit down on one of the sofas, and gracefully sat down across from them. Her crew quietly dispersed throughout the house, yet Diamond could still feel their presence and their guns. Catalina reclined on her sofa, openly looking over Diamond and his companions with her ice-cold stare. Diamond felt displeasure in her stare—she was not fond of their attempt at reconnaissance. Suddenly, a tall and slender youth with classic dark Italian looks appeared out of nowhere carrying a tray with four glasses and a bottle of chilled San Pellegrino. He placed the tray on the low coffee table between them then positioned himself behind Catalina's sofa.

"Diamond, Ferruccio," Catalina broke the silence with an introduction. "Ferruccio, Diamond. And?" she raised her eyebrow at Diamond's friends, waiting for their names. "Sammy, Kevin," they answered. Ferruccio, his hands folded behind his back, simply nodded his head in acknowledgement. Catalina poured the water into the glasses and handed them to the men.

"You know, Eddie could've just called me to find out who was here," she said. "There is no need for sneaking around. Plus, no one can sneak up on this property anyway," she shrugged. Diamond silently nodded in agreement. She took a sip of her water and leaned back on the sofa. "Finish your water, then go back home. Tell Eddie that I'll come and say hello once we're settled in. And, he should just call me next time." She put her glass down on the tray and got up to leave. Ferruccio stayed in his place, Catalina handed him her gun on the way out. He tucked it into the waistband of his jeans, a gesture that was a little too natural for a kid his age noted Diamond. Sammy took a quick sip of his water and put down his glass, elbowing the others to finish as well. He wanted to get the hell out of this house as fast as possible. The three of them jumped up to leave, Ferruccio got the hint and quietly escorted them out.

When the trio got back to Eddie's compound, Sammy and Kevin ran to raid the bar, leaving Diamond to deliver Catalina's message to Eddie alone. Eddie listened with amusement, then shrugged it off. Diamond decided to keep Catalina's displeasure with Eddie's action to himself.

12

New York, SAD

"They're dropping like flies," whispered Campbell to McCarthy. They were holed up in Campbell's cubicle, discussing yet another NOC agent's cover being blown.

"The hits are different. There is no signature," pointed out McCarthy.

"What do you mean?"

"It's a free-for-all. Open season on the CIA operatives. Our guys are on some list, and they're being checked off," explained McCarthy in urgent whisper.

"What do you mean, no signature?" asked Campbell. He was not sure where McCarthy's train of thought was heading.

"Ok." McCarthy peeked above the cubicle wall to see if anyone was listening. But their floor was buzzing with chaos, no one was paying attention to the two of them talking quietly. "I know you think I'm nuts, but hear me out. When the Benedettos do a job, there is a signature. You won't know which Benedetto, but you know it's a Benedetto hit. Their hits are planned to the last detail, calculated, surgical. Their methods are elegant, skillful. There is little to no collateral. They probably stalk their prey for months. They turned killing into an art form."

"A signature…"

"Precisely. These…" McCarthy spread his hand over a pile of files on Campbell's desk, "not an art form."

"So it just means that your little family's not involved," pointed out Campbell.

"No. It means that whoever's issuing orders is not willing to pay for a Benedetto. They either can't afford them, or all this—is for fun. Because if you really had a need to take out a NOC to make a statement, you'll call the Benedettos. But this… this is something else." McCarthy leaned back in his chair, waiting for Campbell to process his words.

"Jesus Christ! Are you thinking this is all just some kind of a twisted game?" Campbell said almost out loud. They both peeked out to see if anyone noticed. All clear.

"And I've got something else for you…" McCarthy pulled Campbell's keyboard over and punched a couple of keys. The deceased agents' names lined up in alpha order. Campbell sat up in his seat—McCarthy got his attention. "Wait for it…" McCarthy said and pulled up a search query. Campbell's clearance was still high enough to look up locations of NOC agents. McCarthy typed in 'Eastern Europe, Middle East' and an identical list of names came up.

"Shit! That's our list!" Campbell realized in horror. He ran his hand through his hair, trying to process what McCarthy just showed him. "Take it down," he finally ordered. "And keep this to yourself for now."

"Trust no one?" inquired McCarthy half-joking.

"Goes without saying," confirmed Campbell, nodding slightly with his chin toward Peel's office. McCarthy nodded. If they could establish that the deaths of their own agents were the result of a CIA leak, and quietly navigate their findings around Peel up the chain of command—it could be the end of Peel and their ticket back into their own Op Room.

13

The Cayman Islands

Pop, and a bright yellow ball arched high above the fence. "Rhheeaahhh!" whined someone and the yellow ball traveled back.

"That's it!" Catalina slammed the cappuccino cup down on the table and walked off the terrace. "Ferruccio!" she summoned.

"*Si, Signora?*" the young man skidded into the room. He took a step back once he saw Catalina's clenched jaw and narrowed eyes. She was not happy.

"Someone's attempting to play tennis next door... Find out who that is," she ordered in a controlled even tone. Ferruccio was not a fan of her calm and even tone of voice, it was usually followed by rapidly fired bullets.

"Tennis?" he asked a bit confused. He had not been outside yet and was not witness to the ear-piercing screeching sounds coming from the property next door.

"*Si, tennis!*" replied Catalina and motioned him to follow her onto the terrace. "There! That tennis!" Catalina pointed with a long and perfectly manicured finger just as another yellow ball made its arc. "I want to have my breakfast in peace and quiet, and I can't because the damn balls are in my field of vision! Not to mention the moaning! It's nine a.m.! Who moans at nine a.m.?" Catalina crossed her arms in anger and waited for Ferruccio's response.

"It's Signora Washington. She plays," Ferruccio offered with a slight shrug. A couple of guys from Catalina's crew snuck over the fence, with considerable ease, to investigate when they heard the whining grunts on the first morning after their arrival. They also knew that the groans and bouncing balls would not sit well with their Capo, who preferred peace and quiet with her breakfast. She lasted longer than they anticipated—three days.

"I'm gonna shove that ball down her throat!" Catalina said quietly, but with enough menace that Ferruccio instantly knew she meant it.

"Or we can just break the machine," he suggested. She gave him a long cold stare before answering.

"Do it! And do something about those basketball games as well while you're at it!" she ordered. Ferruccio nodded and rushed inside, eager to implement her orders.

"Your friend Eddie is a noisy neighbor." That was how Frank explained to her why he moved back to Sicily shortly after discovering that Eddie inadvertently bought the estate next door to his in the Caymans. Catalina wrote off the comment to her father becoming an old curmudgeon. Perhaps her father was mad for not buying the 12 acre estate with its gleaming white house himself, just so no one would move in there. Frank never told her about Seline's early morning tennis practices, nor that an extremely expensive basketball equipment was delivered hanging off a helicopter in broad daylight. The court was built solely for the benefit of Eddie's crew. Just like the tennis court, the basketball court was too close to Frank's fence. He could hear Eddie's crew play almost every evening. They were also noisy players, who sometimes scuffled with each other over the ball and their voices carried all the way to the Bennett house. Frank was annoyed, but never confronted Eddie about it. He simply moved out. He figured that eventually Catalina would visit the Caymans and find out first hand just how large Eddie was living. And that she would take care of the problem immediately. Then, once peace and quiet was restored, he would return back to his Caribbean estate.

After Ferruccio ran off, Catalina stayed on the terrace for a moment watching the bright yellow ball fly from the left side to the right in a perfect arch. "Rhheeaahhh!" and the ball returned. Catalina now recognized Seline's voice. She shrugged in disgust, then suddenly smiled. By tomorrow morning, the ball machine would be in pieces, and as well as the basketball courts. She knew that Eddie was smart enough to get the message that his lifestyle was disturbing her—the equipment would not be fixed. "Swimming, Seline, swimming. You should've picked up swimming, it's a much quieter way to keep in shape," she said in the direction of her screeching friend before walking off the terrace. Downstairs, her crew was already planning their nighttime raid.

14

Seline did not talk to Catalina for a whole week after her morning tennis game was ruined. But finally the loneliness won over and she invited Catalina to spend the afternoon by the pool with her and the kids. The destruction of the tennis and basketball equipment was never brought up—even though Catalina noticed Eddie's men giving her dirty looks behind her back for ruining their favorite evening pastime. She found it amusing. And the fact that Eddie allowed his men to freely roam around the house in the presence of guests—disturbing. She felt that Eddie was being rather lax with his soldiers' discipline.

Seline served Catalina lunch outdoors by the pool so she could watch the children. They dined on Cubano sandwiches, Seline's favorite, plantain chips, and white sangrias. Fresh tropical fruit was served for dessert. The conversation was light and circled around the latest couture and yachts. Seline felt that Eddie needed a mega yacht, Catalina bit her tongue. An arms dealer floating around in a yacht was not a concept she would approve. Half way through her Cubano, Catalina realized she no longer had anything in common with Seline—her friend changed since the move to the Caymans and not for the best. Catalina decided not to do anything about this realization for now.

With lunch concluded, Seline grabbed the sangria pitcher and moved to the chaise lounges by the pool to work on her tan. Catalina reluctantly followed. Eddie appeared to say hello and mentioned that he was about to take a call, but he would join them later. Seline waved him off with slight displeasure and he disappeared into the house.

Catalina and Seline could hear Eddie yelling all the way by the pool. His business call was not going smoothly, it appeared. Catalina looked at Seline and raised an eyebrow in question. Seline shrugged her shoulders and replied that it must be the Mexicans again.

"I think it's an issue of payment," she said.

"Payment? Why is he having problems with payment?" asked Catalina.

"I don't know. I decided not to ask, and I haven't had time to look through his files yet." Seline replied and got up to attend to the children. Catalina took it as a sign that if she wanted to know anything else about this problem, she would have to ask Eddie herself.

Eddie ended the call and yelled out in frustration just as Catalina—a gauzy sarong wrapped around her tiny white bikini—walked through the door of his office and folded herself into a small leather chair in front of his desk. They were quite a sight together: he was furious and sweaty with eyes full of rage, while she was calm and collected. She showed no emotion whatsoever, she just sat there until Eddie's breathing slowed down and he collected himself.

"We told you not to get involved with the Mexicans", she said in a calm and even tone. There it was—we—as in The Family. Right now she wasn't a friend, or a client, or a lethal assassin, she was Capodecina of the Benedetto Family. And she was not happy that he was dealing with a Mexican cartel.

"I had to, or I was going to lose marketshare in South America," Eddie started. She cocked her head to her left, a sign that she was going to give him a chance to explain himself, and shifted into a more comfortable position in the small chair. Eddie leaned back, took a deep breath, and spilled his guts.

She did not interrupt him. She even declined his offer of Bacardi rum with a slight wave of her hand. She sat in her chair, not moving, taking in what he was saying. And she stayed quiet for several minutes after Eddie finished. Then she sat up straight in her chair and looked him right in the eyes. The look was ice-cold. Whatever she was about to say was going to be her, and The Family's, final position on the situation. Eddie has seen this look before—from Don Carlo. Eddie looked down into his glass and put back the contents in one gulp.

"Take him out," she said just as he was about to swallow. He choked and spat out the rum all over his desk. Catalina did not even crack a smile.

"Are you serious? And how is this going to solve my problem?" Catalina did not respond, waiting for Eddie to figure it out on his own. He did.

"Aahhhh… It'll have to be messy." Taking out his troublesome client was simply about sending a message that Eddie did not tolerate being screwed over.

"My cousin would be perfect, but he's taking it easy right now," Catalina was referring to Nunzio's son, the explosive expert. Eddie immediately figured out that it was Catalina's cousin responsible for the Primrose Corporation explosion—a job they all profited handsomely from on the stock market. "I'll do it."

"You don't have time for a setup," said Eddie.

"I don't need a setup. I'll do it long range. There'll be enough left to get your point across," she said. "No charge."

Eddie was secretly relieved when she mentioned 'no charge', her usual fee for a last minute job like that was astronomical. Add another half a mil just because it was in Mexico. She hated that place. Deep down though, a tiny feeling set in that somehow this will cost him a lot more down the road.

"Now, show me the inventory," she unfolded herself out of the chair and motioned him to get up as well. "This needs to be done in less than 24 hours to be effective."

15

Guadalajara International Airport, Guadalajara, Mexico

She took Ferruccio with her at the last moment. Her gut told her that perhaps she should not do this one all by herself. She did not tell anyone, just ordered him to grab his bag and meet her in the car as she was about to walk out the door. Ferruccio was excited, yet extremely nervous. Catalina gave him specific instructions in the car of what she expected of him and how to behave in customs. Then she barely said a word. She wore headphones, yet he knew that there was no music playing, and she only took her sunglasses off for a passport check. Ferruccio watched her, studied her, trying to learn from her behavior. He realized that, unlike him, she was not nervous nor even excited. She was calm, reserved, and very alert.

They got out of the terminal and paused to look for their ride. The instructions for their pickup were very specific: a freshly-washed brand new Mercedes Benz S-class in black, waiting in front of the taxi line with the driver standing outside the car having a smoke. Catalina scanned the traffic in front of her—no sign of the Merc. She walked to the side, Ferruccio quietly following, and stood behind a loud tourist family with mountains of plastic-wrapped luggage. Her height allowed her to see above them with ease. She scanned the cars again—something felt off. Her pick-up was never late. She signaled Ferruccio to stay close with a slight move of her finger. Suddenly, the Merc appeared—it was the right make and model, but it was not as clean as required. Catalina frowned and waited. The car pulled in front of the taxi line, only a lot further than necessary. Catalina waited. Yet, the driver did not get out. This did not feel right. She scanned the taxi line, calculating the possibility of getting a taxi by jumping the queue. Ferruccio got ready to move if she signaled him. Catalina took another look at the S-class, and saw the driver finally get out. He looked tense. He also did not light up. This was a trap.

Catalina quickly ducked behind the loud family, pulling Ferruccio down with her. They swiftly moved toward the end of the taxi line, and then suddenly jumped into the last taxi pulling up. She tossed a couple of hundred dollar bills to the startled driver, gave him her destination and slid lower into the seat. Ferruccio followed her lead and practically rolled himself into a ball on the floor. The taxi passed the S-class, the driver was so busy scanning the crowd, he did not notice it. Catalina took apart her and Ferruccio's phones, then tossed them out the window as the taxi exited the airport. This job was blown.

It took three days for Catalina and Ferruccio to get out of Mexico. And at a significant expense. By the time Catalina walked through her Sicilian villa's doors, she was so wound up that Nonno had to put her under house arrest in order to prevent her from running to the Caymans and blowing up Eddie and everyone else to smithereens. Ferruccio was thoroughly debriefed by Nonno and Luciano, he spared no details—including the tennis court incident.

Eddie, of course, was fully aware of what happened and was promising to clean house and find the traitor. Yet the fact that he was now communicating with Catalina through The Family's Consigliere was a clear sign—he was now living on borrowed time.

Diamond—being a firm believer that one does not bite the hand that feeds him, and spending several restless nights pondering the situation—decided that perhaps it would be best if his allegiances now lay with Catalina. He quietly found a safe house among the locals on the island, and moved his cash and his arsenal from under his mattress to a cavity he made behind a bookshelf in his safe house. He kept his eyes and ears open as he continued with his duties and life as Eddie's top bodyguard and soon started to put together bits and pieces of useful information. Only the picture they painted was rather disturbing.

16

New York

It happened to be an unusually warm March. Around St. Patrick's Day the temperatures jumped to the mid-70s and those that celebrated were forced to dump their Erin sweaters and hit the stores in search of anything green and lightweight.

A rooftop garden on top of a small commercial building sandwiched between loft condos in the Meatpacking district of Manhattan suddenly woke up and filled with tiny budding leaves and early blooms. The hardy perennial herb bushes sprung back to life and were ready to be picked. The garden belonged to the catering company that was housed on the first floor, *A Slice of Heaven*. The garden, the building, and the catering company—the hottest thing in New York at the moment—were owned by a young New Jersey native named Marina Colletti.

Marina Colletti was in her late twenties, cute as a button with brown hair and light blue eyes, and very petite. For such a small and seemingly fragile girl, she had a big and loud mouth. 'I'm an Italian from New Jersey!' was her explanation for sometimes off-color remarks. But her food was amazing, her clients worshiped her, and she treated her staff like gold—no one cared what came out of her mouth. Nick McCarthy met her six months ago when she catered his friend's birthday party and fell head over heels in love. They were now living together in her loft above her catering business, even though the Company did not approve the relationship. McCarthy lied to her about his true job, giving the usual 'I work for the State Department' line, but he had a feeling that she saw right through it.

"I don't like her!" Marina finally said while scraping off plates into the sink. They had just hosted Campbell and his girlfriend, Missy Freston Blackmar, for dinner. In Marina's opinion, the evening was a total disaster. She tried to push Campbell and his girlfriend out the door as soon as the espresso was served, and was now feverishly cleaning up in an attempt to erase any mention of the evening.

"Hey, at least she ate something tonight," replied Nick McCarthy.

"Yeah, a whole fucking carrot! She just pushed the food around her plate pretending to eat. Believe me, I know all the tricks in the book!" Marina pushed the scraps into the disposal, turned on the water, and flipped the switch on the wall with a dramatic gesture. The unit pulverized the garbage with terrifying noise and gurgling sounds. Marina stood over the sink watching the water splatter around before shutting off the disposal with another dramatic gesture. She gave Nick a look before yanking out the garbage can from under the sink and began to toss empty champagne bottles into the can.

"She won't eat, yet she drinks like a fish!" Marina waved an empty bottle of Dom Perignon into Nick's face before dramatically throwing it into the can. "A hundred and seventy bucks a bottle, and the bitch empties out three!" Another bottle flew into the can. "They were for clients, my special reserve, is she going to replace these?"

"She was celebrating," offered Nick. Marina gave him a look of death, tossed the last empty bottle of Dom into the garbage can and stormed out of the kitchen.

"That skinny-ass bitch is not good for him!" She yelled

out while stomping her platform stilettos down the long hallway toward the bedroom. "You have to break them up! Find something that will break them up!"

"I can't," Nick replied quietly. Sooner or later he was going to have to tell her the nature of tonight's dinner with Campbell and his super thin non-eating girlfriend.

"Why the hell not?" Marina was standing in the bedroom door, wriggling around and trying to unzip her dress.

"He proposed..," replied Nick quietly again.

Marina stopped fiddling with the zipper. She slowly lifted her head and stared at Nick. She already took off her shoes and—because of her small stature—had to look up at him, but the look of death still penetrated through Nick's head. She turned on her heel and walked into the bathroom, for once not saying a word. Once in the bathroom, she continued to fiddle with the zipper, Nick still standing in the hall by the bedroom, waiting for her response. Marina finally turned her head toward him:

"Get rid of her," she said slowly and calmly, and in an unusual quiet tone of voice. "Or I'll find someone who will." And she slammed the bathroom door.

Marina and Nick were sound asleep when the front door opened and a male figure slipped inside. The intruder softly closed the door behind him and took two giant steps to avoid the creaking floorboards. He peeked through the vast open kitchen into the hallway leading to the master suite and waited. Silence. He turned and stepped into the library, which was across the kitchen. The small space was defined by floor-to-ceiling built-in black lacquered bookcases filled with books on fashion and cooking, a dramatic contrast to the white sleek interior of the rest of the loft. A camel leather Le Corbusier chaise lounge stood in the middle next to a small round wood sidetable. Nick's open laptop was on the table, to Marina's dismay his notes and papers littered the floor. Nick spent countless hours in that little library pouring over various bits and pieces of intel he gathered on the Benedetto Family. The intruder fiddled with the laptop for a bit then returned it to its original position. He looked down the hall toward the bedroom, before taking large careful steps into the kitchen. He knew where to step to avoid the creaking floorboards, as if he was here before. He reached the enormous marble kitchen island and plucked an orange from a large acacia wood fruit bowl. Marina refilled the bowl right before going to bed. The intruder dropped the orange inside his coat pocket and snuck out the door.

17

The smell of brewing espresso wafted into the bedroom and roused Marina from sleep. She got out of bed and rushed into the kitchen, zeroing in on an enormous bowl of fruit in the middle of the kitchen island. She carefully counted the oranges. Last night, she quietly took a count when she filled the bowl before going to bed, and now one orange was missing. She peeked into the library nook, Nick's laptop was in the exact same position as he left it and his piles of paper looked undisturbed. Marina took a deep breath of relief and busied herself with making a cappuccino.

It was Thursday, market day. On Thursdays, Marina would get up at 4 am, down a cappuccino while showering, and bolt out the door within a half hour, shopping lists in hand. Her stops varied based on who she was cooking for that weekend, and she was always done by breakfast. Today her first stop was the fishmonger—her client wanted an elaborate seafood spread for an 'intimate' group of a hundred people or so. The dealers knew her, she was loud and pushy and always got what she wanted at the price she wanted. They did not mind—when she started out she came with well-connected references. And she always paid cash. Next stop was produce, and she finished off with the meat. She made a quick phone call before starting a heated discussion over the thickness of the filets. By the time she won the argument and counted out the cash, a black Range Rover appeared in front of the meat warehouse and she slipped inside the car as soon as the time of her meat delivery was confirmed. The Range Rover would take Marina to her last destination—an exotic food importer located in the heart of Harlem.

The CIA tailed her a couple of times on market days, all the way to the importer, soon after Nick listed her as 'close and continuing contact'. The import company checked out, but Nick was still asked why they picked Marina up every time and what the actual relationship was. Marina blew up at him after his first cautious inquiry, screaming and gesturing that it was none of his business and all the snooping into her life and her contacts could cost her business and damage her reputation. She stated that the food industry had more secrets to protect than the State Department before tossing Nick's stuff out of their bedroom. That night was his first night on the couch. The next day he informed the Company that he broke off the relationship, then went home to grovel his way back into the bedroom.

This Thursday there was no tail. The Range Rover parked in front of a large brick building with barred windows and dome security cameras on every corner. The driver, a big and lumbering black man with soft eyes and warm smile, got out and escorted Marina to the front door. The door clicked open as soon as she approached and she went inside. The driver remained on the street. There were no markings on the building identifying the business inside except for a small metal plaque above the keypad next to the door. The plaque read: "Washington Enterprises LLC. Exotic Foods Imports."

They met in the conference room. They hugged each other before sitting down to share espresso and bagels with lox from Russ & Daughters, food that he brought with him every time they met. She told him about her morning, he told her about the latest cute thing his toddler daughter did. They chewed their bagels and sipped their espressos, it would be some time before they would get down to business. This was a routine, they met every Thursday for the past six months. At some point he got out his phone and showed some photos of his daughter's outing to the Central Park Zoo.

"Oh, how adorable!" gushed Marina. "Nice stroller! You roll in style!" she commented on the bright red Bugaboo Bee stroller the child was sitting in.

"I can't take credit for that. My sister got it," replied Mark Bennett. "I had a normal one, but she couldn't fold it back when she was out with Sofia one day so she just went and got this one. Probably because it was the most expensive one in the store."

"What did she do with the old one?"

"Garbage? She never told me," Mark answered with a shrug. "She's just like our father, level-headed on the job, impulsive about everything else. When I was young, Dad gutted our kitchen because a cabinet door wouldn't close. I came home from school and there was rubble everywhere. Mom was furious. But two weeks later we had a fabulous new kitchen with cabinets that closed on their own."

"How did you get a new kitchen in two weeks?"

"Well, and I did not know it at that time, Dad put a gun to the contractor's head and told him to be done in two weeks. It worked. Not only was he done on time, but he added bells and whistles we never even knew existed in a kitchen before. He moved to a different state after that though."

"I wonder why…" said Marina with a smile and reached for another bagel. "Maybe I should employ this tactic when my pastry chef is too slow."

"Don't, it's a Benedetto trait you really don't want to inherit."

"How did you find out about the contractor, by the way?"

"My sister told me. She caught on to Dad's business a lot earlier than I did. It's like we were looking at the same thing, only I wasn't seeing it."

"I didn't know my father was a thief until the cops came to the house with a search warrant. Sometimes we see only what we want to see," Marina said quietly. "Should we finish the lox?" They piled the leftover lox on their plates and ate in silence.

"Were you able to get in?" Marina finally asked, since her hands were now free to talk, before putting the last of her bagel into her mouth. She nodded her head toward an open laptop at the end of the table.

"He hasn't turned it on yet," answered Mark. "Once it's on, I'll be able to get in."

"Still sleeping probably. I had to slip him a mickey last night, to make sure he wouldn't hear you. He wasn't falling asleep fast enough," she said. "Do you want me to wake him up?"

"If you can, yeah, that would be great."

"No prob!" She picked up her phone and dialed. "Hey, hon? Can you wake the man upstairs?" she asked her assistant Mike, who was already at work prepping and waiting for deliveries. "Yeah, the noisier the better. And don't forget to check everything as they unload, I don't want any more surprises!" she hung up.

"Problems with deliveries again?" asked Mark.

"Not anymore, thank you very much!" Marina replied with a smile. "But Mike did not check the produce last week and the arugula was all wilted... The fish pulled up while we were on the phone, they're usually obnoxiously loud anyway when they unload and Mike's going to make extra noise. That should wake Nick up. He'll probably jump right out of bed!" she explained and laughed a bit.

"Not much for deliveries, is he?" said Mark. "Any news on Campbell's girlfriend?"

"He proposed! That idiot!" exclaimed Marina, rolling her eyes in disgust. "Nick said he doesn't like her either, but he's not getting involved. Actually… last time I brought it up, he shut me down as usual, but then I caught him mumbling that the only person that could break those two up would have to come back from the grave. Any idea what that was about?" Marina gave Mark a curious look. His eyes narrowed, he stilled for a moment then smiled a bit.

"So Campbell hasn't forgotten… She would be pleased," Mark said with a smile and leaned back in his chair. He was talking about his sister, Catalina, only her name was never mentioned out loud. "She's still hung up on him as well, went all nuts when I told her he was in a serious relationship."

"She's crazy! Did she really think that he would never move on? He thinks she's dead, for God's sake."

"Your boyfriend doesn't. Probably. He's been analyzing every job the Company knows about, looking for clues," said Mark. As if on cue, the laptop beeped. "He's up!" Mark pulled the laptop closer, his fingers dancing on the keyboard. Marina leaned back in her chair and concentrated on her espresso as she watched Mark at work. She knew that at the end of all this pounding, Mark would have a backdoor into Nick's computer and be able to see every file Nick opened. How exactly Mark did it she did not care to know, all she knew was that from time to time he needed physical access to Nick's laptop. 'A black bag job,' he called it. Marina gave him a set of keys. An orange missing from the fruit bowl was Mark's signal that he visited the place—Marina always discretely counted the fruit every night. She was done with her espresso well before

Mark finished his work. He sat there staring at the screen for a while.

"He's not just looking for her, he's trying to track down the whole Family," Mark said finally.

"It's on his own time, he spends hours at home staring at his computer," offered Marina.

"Maybe we can work with this, this obsession could be very useful," said Mark thoughtfully. Marina could see that a plan was forming in his head.

"Do I want to know?" she asked.

"Nope, not yet. I'll let you know if you need to be involved."

They chatted a bit longer about the welfare of her incarcerated father before saying goodbye. She handed him a food list for next week before getting up to leave.

"Just lemons, vanilla, and chocolate?" inquired Mark with amusement after looking at her list. He would leave the list with the one guy that actually handled food for Eddie Washington Enterprises.

"It's getting warmer. Gelato time!" she said with a wink.

As she was exiting the building, the driver was busy loading up a crate of packages into the trunk of the Range Rover. This week's order. The driver looked around to make sure they were alone before placing a rectangular package into back seat. She reached for it as soon as the car got moving and shoved it into her purse. It was a Glock 17 with removed serial numbers and an extra magazine. She wanted to be armed—she had a feeling that her luck was about to run out, and McCarthy was going to find out the truth about their relationship. By providing her with a weapon, the Family was giving her permission to take him down if she ever felt threatened.

18

It was Pai Gow, a Chinese domino game, that was Peel's undoing. He started playing while still in college, mastering the game with ease. He would lose some, then win some, breaking even. Pai Gow was something Peel did to occupy his Friday nights and weekends—he was not a likable guy and the circle of his so-called friends was small. Until he won big in Las Vegas one night.

It was really just dumb luck that he won, and won again, and again. He was drunk, and could not exactly remember the entire night, only that the next day he was invited to a private game of Pai Gow off the strip. The winnings from the night before covered his initial buy-in, and somehow he managed to win at the end of the night. Cheap women and expensive champagne followed him back to the hotel. And so did the invitations to more private games. Suddenly everyone liked him. He was hooked.

He continued to play even as he applied to join the CIA. After the first interview, he was asked to stop if he wanted to move forward with the vetting and interview process. He stopped, but returned to the game soon after his CIA training was over. He jetset all over the world to follow the game, carefully covering his tracks from the Company. Peel was mingling in circles way above his paygrade. It was the lifestyle he craved, the lifestyle he dreamed of. But his spy tradecraft was always shoddy, he never bothered to perfect it or follow the Company's carefully outlined protocols for personal safety. And so he was easily blinded—or carefully misdirected—by the flashy women, the never ending champagne, the caviar. He did not notice that the mix of invited players slowly went from Euro-trash playboys and Russian oligarchs to shady characters from the Middle East, Chinese triads, and finally the Chechen mob. The champagne was replaced by vodka, chilled to perfection. The flashy high-end escorts were replaced by the scared-to-death underage prostitutes from the slave brothels. Peel missed all the clues because he kept on winning. Sometimes not by much, but still winning. And then, one day, he lost.

One does not lose to the Chechen mob, announces that he cannot cover his loses on the spot and walks away with his life. But they let Peel go. For 24 hours. Then, a short and impatient Frenchman, with a garishly dressed blonde on his arm, had his thugs pull him aside just as Peel was about to board his plane home. The Frenchman urged him into a dark booth in the back of an airport bar, and proceeded to explain in detail how Peel was going to pay off his gambling debt to the Chechens. And, at that moment, Peel realized that this was all a set-up from the beginning. From that first night in Vegas, when he suddenly won big—but could not exactly remember how—to the last 24 hours. It was all an elaborate long con to force Peel to work for a Chechen terrorist group. Somehow, somewhere, his shoddy tradecraft failing him completely, Peel must have slipped and disclosed who he was working for. It did not take much effort to verify his story, in his drunken stupor he used a credit card linked to his real identity.

First, the requests were small: a document here, a misdirection of intel there… It went on like this for a couple of years. No one noticed a pattern when the result of Peel's treason led to some kind of operational failure, it was just shrugged off as part of the game. With every exchange

Peel was told about how much his debt was shrinking, he even started to see a small glimpse of light at the end of the tunnel. Then, one day, they asked for the impossible. A list of all the agents working in the old Soviet Block and Middle East. Names, legends, photos, family members—they wanted it all. The price for such delivery? A clean slate. Peel's debt would be paid in full and his service would no longer be required. He said he needed at least six months to put something like this together. They gave him till Christmas.

Peel was just settling into his office chair, careful not to spill his Starbucks, when he heard a faint vibration sound. The phone he kept in his bag was ringing. He ignored it—his coffee and the morning scan of the sports pages were more important than any phone call. "If it's important, leave a message," he said to the bag. The phone soon stopped. Only to start again as soon as he reached for his coffee. Peel kicked his bag in frustration. The phone stopped. He took another sip. The phone started up again. Peel slammed the coffee cup on his desk, spilling some hot coffee on his hand. He swore, and dug up the phone from his bag.

"What!" he barked into the phone, shaking off the scolding liquid off his hand.

"I prefer that you answer carrs better next time," said a falsetto voice with an Asian accent, unable to pronounce his L's.

"Who are you? How did you get this number?" demanded Peel.

"Now, now, Mr. Peer. This is not how you treat your new owner. You have to show respect, or your debt wirr grow," countered the falsetto.

"Debt, what debt, what are you talking about? Who are you?"

"Your friends sord your services to me recentry. I rike your product very much, I need more. You very crever, you cover your tracks very werr. Hee-hee-hee." The little chuckle made the hair on the back of Peel's neck stand up.

"I paid it all off with the last transaction," countered Peel. He carefully looked outside his office to see if anyone was listening.

"No, no. I bought you before you made payment, it is new rures. My rures. Hee-hee," chuckled the falsetto again.

"What do you want?" asked Peel.

"Information, of course. But, I need to find new middre man, since our French friend was kirred on Christmas. Very bad for business, his death, very bad. Your product ferr into many hands before get to me. I wirr carr again soon. You pick up right away now, yes?"

"Yes," gave in Peel.

"Good! We wirr be friends for rong time, hee-hee-hee." The call was disconnected.

Peel wiped the sweat off his forehead. He looked down at his shirt, the sweat stains on his chest and under his arms were spreading. He gulped the rest of his now cooled Starbucks. If anyone were to ask him about the sweaty shirt before he got the opportunity to change, he would blame it on the Starbucks. He counted to ten in his head to calm himself down, then typed in 'Asia' and 'falsetto' as search parameters in the CIA vast database. In the massive list of hits the system spat back at him, there was only one useful result. A dossier of a person of interest named Chen-the-Chin.

19

A sound that could only be compared to a screaming alley cat emanated from the shower. Campbell rolled over in his bed and hid his head under a pillow. But it did not do much to muffle the screeching. Missy Freston Blackmar, his pedigreed fiancé, was belting out a Taylor Swift tune while shampooing her hair. She was rail thin, a tad shorter than Campbell, with a plain thin face and long straight blond hair. Her every feature was long and thin, almost angular. She was Ivy League educated, had a sizable trust fund, and claimed 'fashion blogger' as an occupation. She traveled for her so-called job, which suited Campbell nicely; and name-dropped designers and models du jour in every conversation, which he could not stand but never told her about. Her father was in politics, Campbell met her at some charity social function he had the misfortune to attend and no longer remembered. This morning he was not even sure why he proposed.

The screeching in the shower was followed by the banging of his brand-new vanity cabinet drawers and the slamming of the bathroom trash can lid. For forty-five minutes. 'How could such a small person produce so much noise?' Campbell thought, as he buried his head deeper into the pillow. 'She moves like an elephant!' he quietly groaned. When Missy finally emerged, he pretended to be asleep.

He waited for her to leave before finally getting out of bed. He strolled into the kitchen, naked, to brew a cup of Earl Grey tea. His newly renovated kitchen—all stainless steel top to bottom—was gleaming in the sunlight and smelled like polish. She cleaned. Again. Campbell noticed a wad of damp paper towels by the sink—Missy had a nasty habit of reusing paper towels and she would either hang them on the faucet or collect them in a pile next to the dish sponge. She called it 'being green', he called it 'gross'. Campbell tossed the wet wad into the garbage.

As his tea brewed, he searched his loft for his newspapers. He picked up several European newspapers on the way home last night intending to read them at breakfast. He remembered tossing them onto the glass and chrome coffee table, but this morning the papers were gone. Campbell finally found them in the recycling bin. He swore under his breath and wondered why he was marrying a woman with such an aversion to newspapers. He confronted her about leaving alone his papers at one point, but she simply shrugged and told him to get with the times and get an iPad. When he refused, she gave him one for Christmas.

He liked newspapers. In his line of work, a newspaper was more than a mere source of information: when folded, it was a great place to hide a handgun; its crossword puzzle– a great place to pass on a coded message; even use as jacket padding to make oneself appear fatter or to keep warm. iPads did not keep anyone warm. But then Missy had no idea what Campbell did for a living, nor did she care about current affairs unless it was Fashion Week. Newspapers to her were just a messy nuisance.

Campbell rescued his newspapers and tossed them back onto the coffee table before getting his teacup. As the first sip of hot Earl Grey warmed its way to his stomach, his eyes rested on the staircase to his rooftop deck. The door was bolted with a coded lock, he never allowed Missy to go up there. She was not even aware that the rooftop was completely finished and outfitted with an outdoor kitchen and a hottub. Catalina was the last woman to ever spend time on that roof.

He was still naked when he headed up the stairs, teacup and newspapers in hand. He did not care, he was not going to be flashing anyone. His entire deck was surrounded by a high wooden wall now covered in a blooming vertical garden. He also had several covered areas and trees planted in large containers.

Campbell finished his tea while soaking in the hottub. A small breeze rustled the newspapers he tossed next to the tub, but Campbell was no longer interested in them. His mind wandered back to the night when he had passionate sex with Catalina in this same hottub. He knew now that she was messing with him then, that she knew exactly who he was when she allowed him to pick her up at the Bowery Electric, a night club that he no longer frequented. He knew now that she wore tinted contacts and a wig to disguise her true appearance, but her incredible body was real. He caught what she really looked like in Miami: long dark brown hair and ice cold steel-blue eyes. His gut told him that somehow they were meant for each other. Physically they were perfect together. Even though she drugged him that night in order to clone his phone and slip out unnoticed, it was the best night he ever had. Sex with Missy did not even come close to sex with Catalina. And he knew that there was something more to that night, to their coupling. Because she did not kill him. She shot him up, but did not kill him. Instead she blew herself up.

Chills suddenly ran down his spine as the memory of the boat explosion flooded his head. He cranked up the heat in the tub, took a deep breath and fully submerged. Downstairs, his phone vibrated with an incoming message—he was ordered to Hong Kong by Peel.

20

Marina cooked all of Campbell's meals. She started cooking shortly after moving in with McCarthy, and had Nick deliver coolers full of ready-to-heat meals to Campbell's doorstep once a week. Refusing such a generous offer was not an option. After a couple of deliveries, Campbell simply gave her a key to his place and every Friday she filled his fridge. The food was Sicilian, but Campbell had no idea. All that mattered to him was that it was incredibly delicious, satisfying, and came with reheating instructions in three steps or less. Recently he made it a point to eat something as mouth-watering as a lasagna in front of Missy while she picked at her kale. Slowly, dramatically, rolling his eyes in satisfaction with each bite. Missy would just stab at her kale with more determination. Campbell would finish his meal with a gelato or a cannoli, Missy— by polishing off a bottle of white wine.

Today, Marina had a large cooler on wheels and two big bags overflowing with food. She barely made it through the door. She dragged everything into the kitchen, somehow managing to balance a large Starbucks, her Gucci purse, and her iPhone all in one hand. She carefully put the coffee and her purse on the vast stainless steel kitchen island. It did not take her long to clean out the fridge—she tossed Missy's green juice and tofu in the garbage—and fill it up again. Finished with the fridge, Marina looked for a nice bowl to display the fruit she brought today. Citrus. Straight from Sicily. Right off Catalina's trees. Marina found a large white ceramic bowl decorated with pouty lips around the rim and filled it to the top with gorgeous ripe blood oranges. She smiled as she carefully placed one orange on top of another—if Campbell only knew where they came from, he would choke to death.

The oranges were not part of her usual delivery, they were a rare treat. And, Campbell was completely addicted to them. The bowl would be empty in a matter of days. 'A way to a man's heart is through his stomach,' Marina's mom used to say and Marina was a firm believer of this philosophy. Both McCarthy and Campbell were so well fed, they now required an extra hour in the gym.

With food all put away, Marina checked her watch— just enough time left to carefully snoop around. She did not want to spend more than 15 minutes as not to cause any suspicion. Marina slipped off her stilettos and proceeded to slowly walk through the loft. Campbell remodeled after Catalina's one night visit. Gone were the creaky floors—replaced by wide-planked maple; the newspaper on the windows—they were now meticulously cleaned and left uncovered to the world; all the walls were painted a white custom blend. The kitchen was replaced with industrial-chic stainless steel. The furniture was minimal but masculine and modern. There was an exposed concrete wall separating the bedroom and bath from the main living space. Even the staircase to the rooftop was redone, but it led to a steel door bolted with a coded lock. The only reminder of the previous décor was the enormous television that still dominated the living room.

Marina made her way to the bedroom. The king-size bed was suspended from the ceiling by steel cables, and was dressed in dark Calvin Klein sheets and a fur throw. As usual the bed was unmade. The bathroom was directly behind the bed, separated by a wall of clear glass. There was no privacy, and Campbell preferred it this way. Beyond the bathroom lay a custom closet made out of marine-grade plywood with shiny chrome hardware. Marina headed toward the closet and stopped dead in her tracks.

There were clothes all over the floor. The middle closet cabinet was empty, its contents now laying in a large heap by the closet door. This was unusual—Campbell was not the neatest person in the world, but she never saw clothes piled all over his closet before. Marina carefully stepped over the clothes and made her way toward the now empty cabinet. There was something strange about the back panel. She carefully ran her finger along the edges, then pushed on the panel. It slid open, revealing a large hidden compartment. The compartment housed military clothes with no identifying patches, several handguns, and a pair of combat boots. There was a large empty space on the bottom shelf. Marina leaned down to take a closer look. Judging from the outlines left by a thin layer of dust, a pair of boots and something large was missing. From experience, Marina knew it was a military duffel bag. Her stomach suddenly twisted in a knot. She fumbled with the panel in order to close it, then made her way out of the closet. Campbell was gone on a mission. She needed to know where. She now looked around the bedroom with different eyes—she was desperate for a clue. But she did not find anything.

On the way back out of the bedroom, she suddenly noticed a small note on top of a pile of newspapers on the coffee table. She walked over to see what it was. It was a note to Missy. Marina carefully picked it up by the top right corner to read. It simply said: *Out for a while. Leave the keys on the counter.* Marina could not help but break into a chuckle: if she was reading this correctly, Campbell was breaking off his engagement to Missy. She was about to put the note back, but then noticed that the ink of the pen varied, as if it was written in the indentations made by the writing on a previous sheet of paper. She looked closely and was able to make out a couple of digits. "Well, I guess you'll have to break up with her in person," she said out loud and walked over to the kitchen counter. Marina carefully put the note into her purse, then slipped back into her stilettos. She picked up her now cold coffee and was about to leave, then changed her mind and returned to the bedroom. She put her Starbucks on the nightstand, doused the pillows in Dolce&Gabanna Light Blue perfume she never left home without, and left. "Better than a note," she said out loud, grinning with satisfaction. On the way out the door, Marina walked over to the bowl with oranges and emptied the contents into her cooler. With Campbell not being around to eat them, she did not want the delicious fruit to go to waste.

She called Mark as soon as she exited the building. Three blocks down, she was suddenly picked up by a black Range Rover. She was due back in her kitchen to start prepping for a large party in New Jersey this weekend, but it would now have to wait.

21

Hong Kong, China

Chen-the-Chin was a morbidly obese thug. Weighing over 500 pounds, he ruled from his custom wheelchair by spitting out orders in a falsetto voice while devouring massive amounts of fried chicken, playing countless hours of video games, and watching porn. His upbringing and rise to power in the Hong Kong triads was unclear, there was no trail. It was rumored in the three letter agency circles that he murdered everyone who knew him when he was younger and thinner.

He never made alliances or friends, only enemies. No one willingly worked for him, people were either blackmailed or threatened into submission. There were numerous attempts on his life, yet somehow they all failed. He was the Rasputin of the underworld—he simply could not be killed. The Benedettos would get several contracts on Chen's head a year, yet they always declined. Not that they could not finally put him down, it was simply a business decision—they stayed away from his head, he stayed out of their business.

Chen's greasy fat fingers were in almost all criminal enterprises, from prostitution to murder-for-hire. But what interested him the most was information. He collected every bit of rumor, gossip, tidbit, and secret he could get his hands on. He then used the information in a way that would benefit his purposes the most. Highly-classified American information was of a particular interest to him. In fact, he was obsessed with it. He believed that if he possessed the right secret, it could be traded for American favors that would strengthen his hold in the Hong Kong underworld. Or at least finally to get the secret recipe to KFC's fried chicken, another secret he dreamed all his life to possess.

When the Chechens that owned Peel were suddenly short on cash, they offered their blackmailing business to the highest bidder. Chen-the-Chin pounced on it immediately. His bid was not the highest, but it was cold hard cash instead of the Bitcoin others were offering. The deal was concluded just before Christmas, and the Frenchman was ordered to pass the SD card he collected from Peel to Chen. But the Frenchman's sudden demise at the hands of Catalina spoiled the transaction—and by the time the card finally made its way to Chen, the information it contained was already surfacing in various corners of the underworld and without any discretion or precautions. Chen copied what was of interest to him, then happily traded the card back to the Chechens for an uninterrupted steady stream of fresh slaves for his brothels. With access to the original source—Peel—he finally could get his hands on the top-secret American intel he wanted the most. Chen carefully covered his tracks on the Chechen deal, so no one would steal his prize.

When Chen-the-Chin called Peel, he expected him to be angry at first, then very afraid and defeated— a response he experienced with all of his victims. What he got, however, was Agent Campbell and a wet team. As impressed as Chen was with Peel's ability to mobilize this quickly, it was not a response he anticipated. But, with so many people in his pocket, he was able to alter his plans at the last moment.

22

Sicily

Pop! Said the rifle. And missed the target by three inches to the right. Catalina rolled away from the customized McMillan TAC-338 and hit the ground with her fist in anger. The elusive 2,000 yards shot was still just that—an unreachable goal.

"You need a spotter," she heard Frank's voice in her earpiece. She sat up. Where was he? Catalina looked around to the olive trees surrounding the Field. It was a calm and warm day, the trees provided ample shade to hide under in comfort. There was no point in her looking for her father, he was a master in making himself invisible and Catalina knew it. She lowered herself back into the grass and simply waited for Frank to come over. Soon he was standing over her, looking amused. He was dressed like a farmer—in a linen shirt and rolled-up pants, an old floppy hat covering his head, and a scarf tied loosely around his neck. He was carrying a lupara in one hand and a rifle scope in another. Catalina frowned and pulled the earpiece out of her ear.

"I can't have a spotter," she said to Frank.

"If you want to make this shot, you have to," countered Frank. "A second pair of eyes never hurts, plus you need help with math."

"I don't need help!" Catalina huffed and rolled back around to take position behind her McMillan. Frank dropped his rifle into the grass and plopped down next to her with a grunt. "You're getting old," commented Catalina and adjusted her scope. Frank licked his lips and looked through his own scope, then reached out and made a correction on Catalina's. She gave him a side glance of annoyance but took a second look. She chambered a .338 Lapua Magnum round, aimed, and fired. *Pop!* She grazed the target on the right side.

"Better!" exclaimed Frank. "He'd be missing an arm for sure!' Catalina kicked him in the leg in response.

"I don't play well with others,' she said. "I just need more practice. Maybe I should call Zio Enzo."

"You need a spotter. Someone to verify your math. And to provide cover. Shot like this, no matter how muzzled, is always heard." Frank said after rolling on his side to face her.

"You're too old to come with me," retorted Catalina and sat up. She crossed her long legs and lifted up her arms to stretch out her back. "Nonno never had a spotter," she commented.

"Nonno was a damn good shot, but could never do the math," said Frank and plucked a blade of grass off the ground. "That's why he never did long range jobs. Plus, he preferred to be up close and personal anyway," Frank twisted the blade of grass between his fingers. "Send me Ferruccio—I'll train him."

Catalina paused mid-stretch, thinking. Ferruccio proved rather talented and useful lately. And he tended to stay calm under pressure, or at least able to control his fears. "All right, I'll send him over," she said, and got up to gather her equipment. Frank extended his hand for her to help him up. There was no need to be macho by hiding his age and aching body from his daughter. She pulled him up to his feet, and he waited for her to pack up before asking her to lunch. The Field was not far from his villa, with the right wind he could hear the shots fired.

They walked through the bright green grass toward the olive trees without saying a word to each other. Catalina broke silence to call Nunzio, the boys wanted to use the Field for target practice, and informed her uncle that she was finished for the day. Frank motioned to her to tell Nunzio that he was not home—he did not feel like post-practice visitors today. When Nunzio pressed for Frank's whereabouts, Catalina simply said that he had business with Don Carlo. That always stopped any further inquiries. She pocketed her phone and started walking toward the Mercedes-Benz G63 AMG in metallic jade green that she left under the shade of a large olive tree. She dumped her gear onto a blanket that covered the back seat. Catalina did not want to ruin the white Napa leather upholstery. Frank was about to chastise her for choosing such an impractical color, but decided to keep his mouth shut at the last moment. He climbed into the passenger seat still holding on to his Lupara.

"Couldn't do the math, huh?" Catalina asked suddenly, before putting the car in gear.

"Yeah," chuckled Frank. "When you take over, you might want to double check the books."

"I'm not taking over," Catalina shot back and turned the wheel to zig-zag between the olive trees toward Frank's home. He held on to the grab bar in front of him and watched Catalina clench her jaw in displeasure of him bringing up the Family succession again. She hated talking about it, yet he knew that she did not ask Don Carlo to take her out of consideration. And according to Luciano, there were no other names on the list.

The Field sat in the middle of lush olive and citrus groves. It was long and narrow, and overgrown with grass and beautiful wild flowers. The remains of an old villa still stuck out in the middle and the Field was peppered with holes from various test explosives. It bordered Frank's property on the top, and Nunzio's on the bottom. Nunzio moved his villa to the other end of his land, far away from the Field, in order to have a quiet and safe lifestyle. The Field was the Benedetto's kill zone. In the old days, when they were still carving their own place in *Cosa Nostra*, a lot of their enemies disappeared in this field. Now it was just a training location, Catalina spent her childhood summers there. Don Carlo used to bring her to the Field several times a week, teaching her how to handle various weapons, gradually increasing the distance to target as her skills improved.

The Field was roughly 2,000 yards in length. Catalina had to set up her target right on the edge, and position herself almost in the olive trees. After surviving Miami, she got it in her head that she needed to be able to make the 2,000 yard shot. An impossible shot. A shot only made as a world record eight times. Don Carlo thought she was bored—it was possible for a skilled craftsman to get bored with their skill. Frank thought she was nuts. Antonia, being closest to Catalina and the one she confided to about Campbell after returning to Sicily, thought that Catalina's determination in making the impossible shot was simply a coping mechanism. Every time she fired—she was aiming at Agent Campbell.

They lunched outdoors under the lush shade of mature olive trees on an old wooden table with peeling paint. Frank's villa was the oldest estate in the family, and it came fully furnished. The furniture was old, some of the pieces as old as the villa itself. He did not bother to redecorate, he only replaced or added necessities—like a bed flown in from Harrods London, and a wall of telecom and surveillance equipment sourced from various—sometimes dubious—locations. Frank started to slowly update the plumbing at Catalina's stern insistence. Catalina just could not understand why Frank had not completely remodeled the place, after all it did have really good bones. What no one told her was that this villa was not just the oldest one in the family, this was the house where Don Carlo—and Frank—were born. And Frank was feeling rather sentimental lately.

There was a surprise for lunch—the highly coveted langoustines. The slim, orange-pink ten inch lobsters were flown in live that morning, inside separate enclosures in a cardboard box. The extremely delicious creatures were fragile and temperamental, even looking at each other would drive them into a rage. The langoustines were Frank and Catalina's favorite, and Frank had an unnamed and extremely secret source that he absolutely refused to divulge. Rumor had it the same source also supplied the Bartolota Ristorante di Mare in Las Vegas along with the Russian Duma. Today, these ridiculously expensive and finicky crustaceans were simply grilled and piled into a heap on an old and chipped white ceramic platter to be slowly devoured under the gentle rustling of old olive trees.

Catalina's jaw dropped in surprise when she saw Frank bringing out the langoustines laden platter. His face wore a smug smile of satisfaction. Not much surprised Catalina any more, and Frank made it a point to pull one on her once in a while, even if it meant an early morning air delivery of a certain temperamental seafood. It mattered to him that his daughter was not only alive, but happy. Plus, he loved watching her beg for his source. But some secrets, especially culinary ones, he was planning to take to the grave.

They ate slowly, savoring every single bite. They did not talk, with such succulent food, conversation was unnecessary. Plus, neither of them were much of a talker.

Once the feast was over, Frank and Catalina escaped the sun inside the cooling shade of Frank's covered loggia for a customary after-meal espresso. Catalina stretched out on the couch, fanning herself with an ornate black lace Spanish fan—the abundant food and espresso made her hot. Frank loosened his belt and plopped into an old rocking chair—his favorite spot. He felt some tightness in his chest, but he shrugged it off as heartburn from over-indulgence. The temperature was starting to rise as the afternoon approached, and Frank turned on the overhead fan to keep the air moving. Catalina always came to the Field in early mornings to beat the bright sun in order to avoid strange tan lines, then retreated into the cool indoors. Unlike Frank, Catalina had the luxury to only choose the jobs located in favorable climate with mild temperatures. Frank spent most of his career in various sticky and hot jungles. But then she was smart not to work the CIA contracts.

"Did you hear about that Russian job?" Frank asked Catalina.

"How could you not? It was all over the news!' replied Catalina. "Took six shots to get the job done. Sloppy. And the girlfriend was left alive. Never leave any witnesses even if you're paid to leave witnesses!"

"Well, that's what happens when you use someone in-house," Frank responded with a chuckle. "They should've called us."

"You know how the Russians are: too stubborn and all-mighty to ask for outside help," retorted Catalina. "Such sloppy craftsmanship gives our profession a bad name."

"True, true," agreed Frank. He finished his espresso and looked over at Catalina. She rubbed her elbows, sore and a little red from all the hours spent behind the rifle, her mind on something else. Frank wondered what she was thinking about: was she pondering the mechanics of the Russian job, or did the memory of Agent Campbell suddenly stir up again in her head.

"Penny for your thoughts," he offered. She snapped back to reality and smiled.

"Thinking about my shot, that's all…" admitted Catalina.

"Send me Ferruccio. Then, come back in a day. You'll make progress, I promise."

"Fine. Let's try it your way this time." Catalina got up to retrieve her phone from the car. She was about to dial Ferruccio, when the phone rang. Frank raised an inquisitive eyebrow. 'Nonno,' mouthed Catalina as she answered the call. Frank caught her clench her jaw as she suddenly turned away from him. She did not speak, just listened, and the call was brief. The expression on her face was all business when she was finished. She walked over and leaned to kiss him goodbye. "I gotta go, Daddy," she said.

"Everything ok? What is it, a rush job? We don't do those," inquired Frank even though her facial expression told him it was not a job, but something troubling.

"Not a job. Nonno said it was something I needed to see… No, you're not invited." Catalina immediately cut off any further questions. She grabbed her Spanish fan and quickly walked back to her car. Frank got up to watch her leave. She drove off at high speed, stirring up huge clouds of red dust behind her. Frank waved the dust away from his face and started to clean up the dishes. He wondered if the call had anything to do with Eddie. He knew it was not about Mark, he would have been summoned as well. Finally, Frank decided that the best course of action was to just wait for Catalina to eventually tell him. Or he could just pump Ferruccio for information when the kid arrived. After all, when Ferruccio was not at Catalina's, he was at

Don Carlo's. An hour later, Ferruccio gently knocked on Frank's door and quietly asked to come inside. Whatever was going on, Catalina had enough time to send him over. Smiling broadly, Frank welcomed in the young man with open arms.

23

New York

'How could something so well planned go wrong so fast?' incomprehension tugged on McCarthy's mind. He tried to pick up his drink, but his hands could not stop shaking. He needed a drink badly. He managed to wrap both hands around the glass, and willed them to stay still just long enough to bring the glass to his lips. McCarthy downed his double shot of Powers in one gulp. The amber liquid spread quickly, and his hand shook a little less. The bartender materialized in front of him with a refill.

It was supposed to be a simple grab job. Get in, get out. They had reliable intel, verified through multiple channels. Small team, two vehicles, light tactical gear. Put down Chen's bodyguards, take him in his own van. They had a small window of time, but with Campbell in charge, no one was worried about the execution. 'What the fuck happened?' McCarthy screamed in his head. His hands were still shaking.

The black Suburbans they used had small cameras mounted on the dashboard. The team was wearing comm equipment. However, the view the cameras provided was very limited, and for some unknown reason they were also unable to tap into the CCTV feed of the building. The group of people assembled in Peel's Op Room were forced to rely on their own expertise and imagination in order to fill in the gaps between muffled one word communication of Campbell's team and the live feed. At the beginning, everything seemed to go as planned. For about five minutes. Then, all hell broke loose. There was gun fire, lots and lots of gun fire. Campbell and his men were ambushed. They had no way out. Chen-the-Chin was nowhere in sight. The team used the Suburbans for cover, but one of the dashboard cameras was shot to smithereens almost immediately.

There was shouting. Screaming. More shouting. In New York, Peel's men scrambled for any visuals, trying to grab feed from any available surveillance systems in the target area. Suddenly it was all over. New York watched in horror, through the remaining Suburban camera, as the bodies of Campbell's team were dragged into one pile for display. A couple of men were fatally wounded—they were shot to death on sight. And then, a large well-armed shape lumbered over to the Suburban and ripped out the camera, cutting the feed. The show was over.

New York counted the bodies and ran facial recognition. One was missing. Campbell. Peel was about to send in an extraction team to a designated rendezvous location, but McCarthy stopped him. There was no need: Campbell would not abandon his team, the only reason he was not in the pile of bodies was because he was captured.

McCarthy wrapped his fingers tightly around his glass and downed his drink. His hands shook a little less and his shoulders started to release some tension. He motioned to the bartender for another.

The bar, inside Locanda Verde restaurant in Tribeca, was starting to fill up with the post-work crowd. Millennials huddled together by the bar, drinking signature cocktails, engrossed in their phones instead of conversations. McCarthy was attractive: tall, fit, with light brown hair and warm grey eyes. And in his current disheveled state he looked down right irresistible. Yet, he was completely ignored by a flock of Ivanka Trump wannabes, too consumed with swiping right on Tinder looking to score a quick hookup. Which suited McCarthy just fine. The bartender was a close friend of Marina, their friendship was why McCarthy ended up here—he needed the safety of a familiar face that would not ask any questions. Another double shot of Powers materialized in front of him. His hands less shaky now, he took a long sip.

He was surprised when he was not listed as part of Campbell's team. He felt hurt, even though he understood, when Campbell refused to take him along. "I need a friend in that Op room," was how Campbell explained his decision, "I need someone I can rely on. And you're it." McCarthy promised Campbell a drink once his friend was back stateside. As he watched the slaughter of Campbell's team—digging his fingers into the back of someone's chair he happened to stand behind, his knuckles turning white, as he tried to control himself in a helpless situation where he could do absolutely nothing—his mind screamed 'Fuck, that could've been me! Right now, I would be dead!' Now, staring into his drink, all he could think was 'I'm alive, I'm alive, I'm alive.' He owed Campbell his life. He swirled around his whiskey and took another swig.

The image of Peel, collapsing into a chair in utter disbelief of what they just witnessed, appeared in McCarthy' head. McCarthy had no recollection of how he left the Op Room, his feet carried him aimlessly around the streets of New York, until he came to in front of Locanda Verde. He was shaking all over. Unable to go home in such a state, he pulled the heavy door open and managed to get himself to the bar. Locanda Verde had just opened for the evening, there were no customers yet. The bartender took one look at McCarthy and poured him a double shot of Powers, McCarthy's favorite whiskey, without saying a word.

McCarthy left Peel slumped in the chair, absently mumbling to no one "I don't understand… That's not what I planned… How did he know?.." Peel's mumbling swirled around in McCarthy's brain, setting off tiny alarms he was too numb to understand yet. He kept drinking to drown out Peel's mumbling.

<Come and get your boyfriend, he had a rough day> texted the bartender to Marina late at night.

<On my way. Close the tab> responded Marina. A short time later, she walked into the bar—in an oversized sweatshirt emblazoned with 'Cindy Crawford' in block letters, leggings, Uggs, no makeup, and extremely large hoop earrings—and pulled up a chair next to McCarthy. She dug out her credit card from her Gucci purse, as the bartender approached with the bill. "Did he say much?" she mouthed to her friend. "No," he mouthed back and shook his head. Marina breathed a sigh of relief.

"Hi Hon!" she said quietly to Nick. "Ready to go home?" He looked into the bottom of his empty glass and nodded 'yes'. Marina signed the receipt, adding a very generous tip, then slid off her chair to help Nick off his. She needed to support him on the way out the door.

Back home Marina poured Nick into their bed and he passed out as soon as his head hit the pillows. She snuck back downstairs and turned on a red heat lamp in her catering kitchen. Visible through the window, it was a sign to Mark Bennett to stay away. Tonight was not a good night for unannounced visitors. She tiptoed back upstairs and snuck into bed next to Nick.

Hours later, Nick woke up, panting, short of breath. Nightmare. He was covered in a cold sweat. Campbell saying 'I need a friend in that Op room' bounced around in Nick's head. He shook his head to wake himself up fully, to chase away the nightmare. In his dreams, he relived Campbell being shot up in Miami, only to then recover long enough to be brutally tortured by a fat ugly creature. Nick got out of bed. He stumbled into the bathroom to take a cold shower. In the shower, finally regaining his composure, he vowed to himself that he would make sure his friend was rescued. No matter what the cost.

24

Amalfi Coast, Italy

The astonishing 390 foot mega motor yacht, simply named B, lay off shore on the Amalfi Coast for a week. Its gleaming white futuristic design, a cross between a submarine and a stealth ship, made a jarring visual statement against the old picturesque stone buildings clinging to the steep shore and narrow winding roads of the Amalfi Coast. The owners disembarked shortly after the arrival to stay at a villa they owned in Positano. But they were of no particular interest to anyone anyway. It was their guest that stayed onboard who, unbeknownst to himself, was of a significant value to a certain interested party.

His day started just like any other onboard B: sex, full breakfast, more sex, relax in the hottub on the top deck. He slathered himself with tanning lotion and trotted out to the hottub. A group of scantily-clad, extremely thin, and super young Hamptons socialites clustered around the covered bar taking selfies. He grabbed an ass in passing, but there was not much there to hold on to. 'I should take them all to Mexico for ass implants,' he snickered to himself as he climbed into the tub. A steward came over with an offer of cigars, he lit one up then closed his eyes and floated in the water. Or rather attempted to—he was too big and bulky to actually float. The day was gorgeous with not a cloud in the sky above them.

Don Carlo called this type of job a quickie. Get in, take care of a target, go home. All in less than 24 hours. "Go pull a trigger, clear your head," said Don Carlo to Catalina when he tossed the dossier into her lap. He called her in to inform her that Campbell had been captured by Chen-the-Chin.

"How do you know?" inquired Catalina after swallowing the news.

"I've been keeping tabs on Chen. A botched-up CIA Black Op is hard to miss," answered Don Carlo. He omitted the fact that Mark informed him earlier that Campbell was in Hong Kong. He perched on the edge of his desk, Catalina found a seat by the fireplace.

"You're a son of a bitch—you've been playing the market with Chen's head!" she snapped back.

"Oh please! You would do the same and you know it!" retorted Don Carlo. He was waiting on the price on Chen's head to climb past seven figures before finally considering the contract. "What do you want to do about your agent?"

"Don't know. See how it plays out? And he's not my agent," responded Catalina in a controlled tone.

"Here," Don Carlo looked through the files on his desk, "take this one. You should be working, not sitting around."

It was a beautiful sunny day. The Tyrrhenian Sea was sparkling brightly under the sun. There was too much reflection off the water for Catalina's liking, but the mega yacht was hard to miss. She looked through the scope of her McMillan TAC-338, her rifle of choice lately, and found her target lounging in the hottub on the top deck in a tiny bright orange Speedo. She picked up on a small group of topless coeds guzzling rosé by the bar. For moment she considered whether or not they could pose a problem for her, but then noticed that they were more interested in the bartender and his rosé-pouring skills than her hottub target. She checked on her range again, just a little over 1000 yards. Through the open window, Catalina heard a faint whine of a motorcycle outside. The sound was moving closer. She chambered her round and wiggled her body into a more comfortable and steady position on top of a dining table. The motorcycle whine was quickly approaching, followed by several car horns. She put her finger on the trigger and steadied her breathing. The motorcycle was getting closer, the whine louder. The moment the offending motorcycle accelerated right under her open window, she fired. The suppressed pop of her McMillan was covered by the sudden whine of the motorcycle. The bullet sliced through the air, traveling over azure waters, and punched a hole in the target's chest. The cigar fell out of the mouth and he slid under the water. The rosé and selfie party by the bar did not even notice.

Catalina put away her rifle, pushed the dining table back to its position in the middle of the room, and closed the window. Outside, she loaded herself into a white red-roofed Fiat 500c Cabrio and carefully merged into the chaotic traffic. As she was about to exit the city limits, the familiar whiny motorcycle caught up with her. The motorcycle weaved its way between cars and pulled up extremely close to the Fiat. Catalina rolled down her window and handed the biker a fat envelope. He slid it inside his black and red leather jacket and sped away. Catalina rolled up her window and found a fun dance tune on the radio. Don Carlo was right: the quickie did clear her head.

25

Hong Kong, China

The tiny room Campbell was confined in was the most bizarre place he had ever seen. Every square inch was upholstered in purple velvet that had seen better days and was tufted with gold nail heads. A gold-framed mirror covered the entire wall across the tiny bed—Campbell figured out instantly that it was a two-way mirror. The tiny bed was too small for Campbell and was made with leopard-print silk sheets that most likely had never been washed. The first night after he was dumped in this room, he stripped off the bedding, flipped the mattress and dragged it on the floor. He was used to sleeping on a mattress on the floor and that way he could stretch out. It was also a way of showing to his captors that he was still in control of himself.

There was no window, the only light was provided by pink rope lights embedded in a shape of a naked woman into a smoke-mirrored ceiling. There was a sink with gold taps, a bidet and a toilet. The sink faucet dripped, slowly and constantly. A large stack of toilet paper rolls was piled almost to the ceiling next to the toilet, something else that Campbell found bizarre.

On the wall with the two-way mirror was the door to the room. It was upholstered in purple velvet just like the walls and had no handle. The door was extremely narrow in width but very tall. There was a peephole and a small pass-through by the floor that was used to slide food into the room. Food was delivered once a day at random times. The menu was always the same: several pieces of fried chicken, chips, and a small orange soda. The plates were foam and no utensils were given. Campbell would dump out the soda and fill the bottle with water. No one stopped him.

Every time the food came, Campbell felt that he was being watched. So one day, when the food arrived, he sat on the floor with his back to the mirror. Immediately there was an impatient tapping on the other side of the mirror, he ignored it. A minute later, the door opened and two bulky thugs squeezed themselves in, grabbed Campbell off the floor and pushed him onto the bed. They placed his plate on his lap and, in broken English, ordered him to look at the mirror and eat. Slowly. So, someone on the other side of that mirror liked to watch people eat. Fried chicken of all things. Campbell remembered seeing in Chen-the-Chin's file that he was obsessed with fried chicken and had to have it at every meal. Which meant that Chen-the-Chin was on the other side of the mirror.

At first the torture wasn't physical. It was psychological. First there was isolation and the ever-dripping faucet, which Campbell deduced was intentional. The slowly dripping water was disturbing his sleep pattern, he had a hard time staying asleep. It might have been a week or possibly longer before the noise started. Campbell was finally asleep for several hours when the noise burst into the room. It sounded as if a war was going on all around, he heard explosions, weapons firing, people screaming. 'Thank God!' thought Campbell and jumped to his feet. He thought he was being rescued. But minutes passed, yet no one burst through the door. In the back of his mind, a thought appeared that the sounds seemed familiar. He tried to shake it off and hold on to hope that this was indeed a rescue, but the nagging thought did not go away. Instead it grew larger and larger until it filled his brain and forced Campbell to pay attention to the screams behind his door. It did not take him long to realize that the sounds were not from an actual fire fight going on outside his room, but from a *Modern Warfare* video game. There was no rescue. He slumped back on the mattress in despair. The game sounds were followed by the blasting of bad 80's music, so loud that Campbell stuffed toilet paper into his ears in a futile effort to muffle the sound. When the music finally stopped and the quiet returned, he had a migraine that lasted for days. Then the beatings started.

26

New York

As promised, the second video of Campbell being beaten into a pulp came exactly 48 hours after the first one. Again, they were forced to watch Campbell take a beating before Chen-the-Chin's falsetto voice demanded that the Company turn over the details on a long list of assets in exchange for Campbell's life. And again Peel refused, citing that the US government does not negotiate with terrorists. Chen-the-Chin again gave them 48 hours to think it over, but warning that he was not a patient man before hanging up. McCarthy immediately demanded that they send in a team to rescue his friend, but all he got in return was the 'we're looking into all possibilities' speech. He realized that the Company was disavowing Campbell. But McCarthy, even though he was a loyal Company man, just couldn't toss away his friend and mentor like a piece of used trash. He had to do something. He only had one card left to play, and it was just a hunch, but he was a desperate man looking for a desperate measure. He knew that it would end his career, and possibly his own life, but there was just no other way. He stormed out of the building and ran home. It was just before lunch hour, if he hurried, he could catch still Marina.

The black Gucci edition Fiat 500, sporting vanity plates LILRVOL, took a sharp turn and flew into the garage. The car halted to a stop just an inch shy of hitting a large pile of storage boxes. Marina waited for the garage door to completely close before exiting the car. She did not want anyone to see that she was armed. She pulled up the passenger seat cushion to reveal a hidden compartment where a Glock and several extra magazines were stored. She emptied the compartment, fitted back the cushion, and popped a full magazine into her Glock. The last thing she did before exiting the Fiat was to remove her large hoop earrings and drop them into the cup holder. Girls bred in New Jersey always took off their hoops before getting into a fight. Whatever was waiting for her inside, she was now ready.

A couple of hours prior—during a meeting with an old family friend and a client in New Jersey—Marina got a frantic call from Mike, her sous chef, saying that Nick was home and was acting very strange and asking for her. Mike added that it sounded like Nick was tearing their loft apart, as if he was looking for something. Marina's heart sunk. The game was over… She ordered Mike to get the staff out as fast as possible. And quietly. Mike was worried about the food, she told him to forget it. She politely excused herself from her meeting citing a kitchen emergency and ran to her car.

Her immediate stop was a convenience store for a burn phone. She then slipped into the bathroom, broke apart her iPhone and flushed it down the toilet. As she sped down the George Washington Bridge toward Manhattan, Marina called Tyrone. A long time ago, she was instructed to do so if she thought she was blown. Tyrone handled Eddie's stateside businesses and had gotten extremely close with Mark. As soon as she told him what was going on, he immediately offered her guns and muscle and insisted that she run. She declined both, but asked that if she did not check in at the end of the day, he was to hunt Nick down like a dog. Tyrone reluctantly agreed after he detected the 'don't mess with a Benedetto' tone in her voice. He heard the same tone before—from Catalina in Miami.

Marina dug through her Gucci bag for her address book as she tried to keep her eyes on the road and steer with her left hand. She finally found the book and used her left leg to hold the steering wheel straight while frantically paging through the tiny book for a number. She found what she was looking for under 'pest control' and dialed.

———

Bagheria, Sicily

Luciano Benedetto always carried three phones: one for the Family, one for everyone else, and one with a U.S. number. The U.S. phone never rang. Until today. He was enjoying a lovely dinner outdoors but, since the phone never rang, did not recognize the ring. The U.S. phone had no voicemail so it just kept on ringing. Puzzled, Luciano checked out his other two phones, but found them silent. Alarmed when he finally realized that it was someone from the States trying to reach him, he finally found the little slim device screaming away in his pant pocket. He did not recognize the number.

"Yes?" he answered with caution.

"Segnior Benedetto? Is my Daddy safe? Is he ok?" a strong female voice with an East Coast accent demanded. Luciano immediately knew it was Marina Colletti. But the fact that she called him directly asking about the well-being of her imprisoned father—who was under Benedetto's protection—was a great cause for alarm. Luciano sat up straight in his seat.

"Yes, Marina, he is safe."

"You make sure he's safe. And you tell him that I love him."

"Marina, was is going on?" Usually calm under pressure as all Benedettos, Luciano's blood pressure was starting to rise slowly.

"The shit's about to hit the fan, that's what's going on! Nick knows! He knows!" Marina screamed into the phone. Luciano heard her take a deep breath in an attempt to calm herself down, before she filled him in on the conversation with her sous chef. She also told him that something serious must be happening in the Company because Nick had not been home for the past three days.

"Marina, run! Do not go back home!" Luciano ordered.

"No! I need to know what he knows. I'm armed and I'm not going down that easy!" she answered. Luciano heard a car horn, followed by the most colorful sentence ever uttered by a female. Marina was driving, he figured. "Look, I need to hang up here," she was back. "Keep my Daddy safe and this makes us even. *Capisce?*"

"*Sí*," Luciano could not help but crack a tiny smile as Marina's New Jersey Mafia upbringing showed through. She hung up. Luciano immediately reached for his Family phone and dialed Catalina.

New York

She checked on the kitchen first, before going upstairs. There was not a scrap of food anywhere, Mike must have managed to put everything away. He left all the mixers on, they provided enough noise to give the illusion that the kitchen was bustling with activity. 'Smart man,' remarked Marina to herself before slowly ascending up the stairs. She found the door to her loft wide open, the inside dark and gloomy. Nick had pulled the blinds closed. She could not see him. Marina took a deep breath, drew her gun, and entered.

He heard her walk in, but couldn't really make her out in the dark. He did not notice that she was packing. He let her walk all the way to the dining table before he emerged from his perch in the library and flipped on the lights. She spun around and he came face to face with a Glock. He was surprised, but managed not to show it.

"Who are you?" he asked her.

"You know who I am," she replied. "I'm Marina Coletti, caterer to the stars and your girlfriend," she sassed in order to regain her composure.

"What's your connection to the Benedettos?" he asked after a long pause. She raised an eyebrow, but did not respond. "Let me rephrase that—who is your contact for the Benedettos and how do I get in touch?"

"I don't know who you're talking about," Marina said calmly.

"Drop the act, honey! I know you're mobbed up! No one has a cushy gig like this without the mob!"

"Are you fucking kidding me? You think you've figured it all out! You're not getting anything! I'm the one with the gun here!" She shifted her body and assumed a proper firing stand. Nick did not move, nor say anything. He just stood there looking down the barrel of her gun for a while, then made a sigh and she saw his shoulders slump. She had seen this before, he was giving in.

"Jim's been captured… And the CIA is not going to do anything about it… I can't just leave him there… I need to get him out… I need help… I just thought that maybe the Benedettos… this is my last resort…" he was talking very softly, she could barely make it out. She wanted to drop her gun and pull him into her arms and tell him that everything will be OK, but she did not. She just stood there, with her legs apart and her back straight, holding the gun in both hands, looking him over, trying to figure out if this was all a bluff. But he just looked broken, sad, hopeless. Marina realized that this was real.

"What makes you think that they'll help?" she asked.

"Because I don't know anyone else outside the CIA with enough skill to pull it off," he answered, a glimmer of hope flashing in his eyes. "Look, I know he killed a member of their Family, and they can refuse me, but I need to ask! Please!" Marina lowered her gun and motioned him to sit down on the couch. She remained standing. "Where is he?"

"His last known coordinates were in Hong Kong. Chen-the-Chin's got him." Nick assumed, correctly, that she knew who that was.

"Shit… I need to make a call," she said and pulled the phone out of her jacket pocket. "He's asking for access… It's about Loverboy… Yep, not a problem!" the conversation was short. "Come on, we gotta go. I've been instructed to bring you in," she motioned to the door with her gun.

She made him leave his phone in the downstairs kitchen when she stopped in to turn off the mixers. Nick was surprised to see that no one was there. She tied a scarf around his eyes before he got into the car and turned on Bruce Springsteen full volume as soon as they pulled out of the garage. They drove for quite a while, with lots of sudden left and right turns. Nick realized that Marina was trained in evasive driving and that the loud music was to cover up any possible street noise that he might have picked up on. She did a really good job, by the time she finally announced that they arrived he had no clue where they were.

She helped him out of the car, still blindfolded, and led him into a building. Or a warehouse, he could not tell. He heard a heavy door open and close with dull thuds, then something rolled along the floor. Marina gently pushed him to sit down, he landed into a comfortable office hair. Then, she finally took his blindfold off.

He was in a windowless conference room with a long table, leather chairs, top-notch telecom equipment, and a large TV hanging on the wall. The TV was on, but displaying nothing. Marina sat next to McCarthy, then checked something on her phone. She sighed then stretched in her chair.

"What now?" prodded Nick.

"Now we wait," she said and yawned. "Our time zones don't exactly align. Someone has to be woken up to take our call and that's not exactly a pretty picture. Or a safe one, for whoever is unlucky enough to do the waking." She snorted a little, privately laughing at an inside joke, and closed her eyes to take a nap. Nick, unable to contain himself, got up to pace around the room.

Marina was woken up almost an hour later by a ping of the phone that she was still holding in her hand. She checked the incoming message and motioned Nick to sit back down. She typed something back, the incredible speed of her thumbs still amazed Nick. He sat back into the chair. Marina sat up in her chair, checking her phone. She waited a bit, then checked again. And again. Waiting for a response, Nick realized. Finally, the phone pinged.

<You can tell him> the text said. Marina took a deep breath and leaned back in her chair. "Nick?" she started, turning her chair slightly toward him. "That day in Miami… Jim did not kill anyone."

"What are you talking about?" he asked. 'How did she know about Miami?' he thought. Nick suddenly got a bad a feeling.

"You and Jim, you did not kill anyone. Wounded, yes, but did not kill."

"I'm not following you. The boat… it blew up. I watched it blow up! No one could have survived that!"

"She did," Marina responded calmly, as if they were discussing what frosting to put on cupcakes. "Catalina's alive, Nick. And she's about to take your call." She dropped the bombshell and got up to leave the room, just as the large screen on the wall lit up to reveal the face of a very beautiful woman. McCarthy instantly recognized who she was, that face was forever ingrained into his memory. He stared speechless at the screen, forgetting for a moment why he was here. Catalina Bennett was very much alive. And he was about to ask her to rescue a man who pumped her full of lead in Miami a year and a half ago.

27

Provincia di Palermo, Sicily

"So there is no other way in?" asked Catalina. Her fingers drummed on the stainless steel frame of her PixelSense table.

"Not unless you're SEAL Team Six, and look how that worked out," answered Frank, referring to Campbell's failed operation. McCarthy told Catalina that Campbell's team attempted to enter the building from the ground, which turned out to be a lethal mistake.

The table was displaying the floorplans to the Hong Kong tower Chen-the-Chin called home for the past several years. Because the Benedettos were getting contracts on Chen's head on such a regular basis, they had amassed quite the dossier on him, including the floor plans to the building. The only things they were missing were the blueprints to the floors that belonged to Chen. Catalina zoomed in with a swipe of her hand and studied the plans more closely. Her father was right. As usual.

"Well, since there is no other choice... Ok, fine. But I hate jumping!"

Don Carlo pushed the plate with a couple of still-steaming octopi toward Luciano and walked to the window to watch the taillights of Catalina's Mercedes G63 disappear down his gravel driveway. She came to get his blessing before taking off. After sitting down with her in his office to go over her operation—again—and giving her some solid and much appreciated advice, he finally gave her his blessing. She had a bit of time to enjoy a small meal with him. Luciano, Don Carlo's Consigliere, joined them half way through.

"Why is she doing this?" asked Don Carlo.

"Because she was asked to?" Luciano wondered, perfectly knowing that it was not the right answer.

"No."

"They fit each other perhaps," speculated Luciano.

"They're from different worlds, it will never work."

"I guess we'll just have to wait and see." Luciano walked over to stand next to Don Carlo by the window. He brought the plate with leftover octopi and offered them to his Don. The offer was first waved off, but Luciano knew his Don all too well and did not move. Don Carlo stared at the delicious purple tentacles for a while, then picked one up with a shrug. Luciano smiled and retracted the plate.

"I wonder what her execution will be, will she do it with stealth and finesse, or will she start a war?" pondered Don Carlo.

"Probably depends on how she feels when she lands. She hates operating in Hong Kong, says it smells."

"Like fried chicken!" Don Carlo let out a laugh. Luciano followed him with a little chuckle.

"Her Cayman friend would love it if she started a war, he needs the business."

"Her friend needs to be looked into," Don Carlo said after a pause. It was an order.

"And whose idea was this, may I ask?" Luciano never questioned his orders, but this time he was curious.

"Catalina's. She said he's not as careful as he should be. And after Mexico, she's even more suspicious."

"Good. She's learning… Making the right calls." Luciano nodded with pleasure. "This is good, very good." He turned to leave. "I will need some time to make the report."

He said to Don Carlo before opening the door.

"Don't leave any stone unturned. Report to Catalina when you're done. And take your time. If she succeeds with this 'little' rescue, she will most likely be occupied for quite a while," instructed Don Carlo. Luciano left the room, silently closing the door behind him.

28

Hong Kong

By the time Catalina cleared the top floor and silenced two of Chen's henchmen, with a clean and efficient slice of their throat, her heart returned to its normal low and steady rate. As much as she hated jumping out of planes, especially at high altitude, the roof was the only easy way into the building. There was no way to discretely land a chopper or even get one near the tower; Chen had the airways secured through a long chain of blackmail and bribery. The rooftop was not guarded under the assumption that there was no other way to access it. No one considered that someone might just be crazy enough to parachute in.

Chen-the-Chin's lair consisted of several top floors of the One Island East skyscraper in Hong Kong. His residence in the building was shrouded with secrecy. When the 69 story glass tower was damaged by the tropical storm Kammuri, Chen seized the opportunity to make large scale improvements of his own. Unbeknownst to all other tenants, he had full control of the building by the time the repairs were complete.

Catalina had almost finished dragging yet another body into a dark corner when she noticed that, suddenly, all the CCTV cameras started to randomly pan side to side, as if looking for something. 'Shit,' she thought. She was spotted. There was no more time for a stealthy and slow approach, she now had to move quickly. Catalina wiped the blood off her ceramic knife on her victim's pants and holstered it. The dead body in front of her was armed head to toe, but as tempting as it was to use his weapons to reserve her ammo, hers were already fitted with suppressers. She drew her guns and proceeded to clear the floor.

She left behind three more bodies, each with a pair of bullets in the chest, and disabled CCTV cameras as she slipped into the emergency stairwell to descend to the floor below. With two floors cleared and a rising body count, she had yet to locate Campbell. Catalina told herself that if she failed to find Campbell on the floor she was about to enter, then she could start panicking. She took a deep breath, positioned herself ready for an assault, and slowly cracked the door. With no one immediately shooting at her, she carefully slipped inside. And stopped dead in her tracks. This floor was different.

Here, the ceilings were much higher than the previous two floors she left behind. The hallway was wide, running in both directions, and divided at regular intervals by large square columns that supported the ceiling. And every surface, except the floor, was mirrored. The floor was tiled in large slabs of white-veined black marble. Couches, tufted in purple velvet, encircled each column. The space was dimly lit by rope lights snaking along the walls in intricate wave patterns. The hideous décor reminded her simultaneously of a bad strip club mixed with an airport terminal designed in the 80's.

Catalina moved against the wall, trying to get as flat as possible, and carefully looked around again. All these mirrors were a tactical nightmare, she would have to just shoot first and think later. To the left, the wide hallway seemed to turn, or contain a passage of some sort; to the right, it dead-ended into a large mirrored wall lined with colored glass vases and figurines standing on marble pedestals. The wall she was leaning on was smooth, but the wall across her was different. It seemed to contain more panels. She squinted slightly to try and figure out what was on that wall. And then it hit her—doors. The entire wall was lined with doors.

She decided to move left to see if that dark hallway turn was going to pose a threat when she noticed dark shapes reflecting in the walls and rapid fire suddenly surrounded her. She dropped on the floor and followed the trajectory to its point of origin. She unloaded a full magazine and rolled toward the couch for cover. Her dark clothing blended her well with the purple couch and the black marble floor tile. She heard a low groaning sound, then something hit the marble with a thud. Unlike her opponent, she did not miss.

Crouching, she made her way toward the body that was splayed on the floor. He was blocking a mirrored door that seemed to swing both ways. She pushed the door in— it was a bathroom decked out in black marble with gold taps shaped like swans. Catalina dragged the motionless body inside, and reloaded. She needed to start making her way through all the doors.

The first door she hit was unlocked. Catalina pushed the door wide open. Behind the door was a tiny room upholstered top to bottom in purple velvet. There was a small bed with a stained mattress, a sink, and a toilet. The room had an unpleasant stale odor of urine and fried chicken. Catalina left the door open and moved on. She cleared the next room that looked and smelled exactly the same, when she heard a ding of an elevator down the hall. She ducked inside the room, and closed the door behind her almost all the way. She was able to see just enough through the crack she left open. The elevator's doors slid open and slowly two short men stepped out, their guns drawn. But Catalina had the upper hand and she quickly put them down with two shots to the chest. As she slowly and quietly approached the elevator, suddenly a spray of fire rang out from the inside. She hit the floor. She checked the mirrors surrounding her, looking for them to give up the shooter. There he was, crouching inside the elevator, waving his Beretta nervously from side to side. Catalina made her way to the elevator and put him out of his misery with a perfect shot to the head. She got off the floor, and dragged the two bodies inside. She left one half way out, to block the doors from closing and thus disabling the elevator. She noticed that the last shooter had a fresh cut between the thumb and the index finger, a tell-tale sign of improperly handling a handgun. "Beretta bite," said Catalina and rolled her eyes. "Amateurs!"

So far, her search of the floor was providing no results. Door after door revealed identical rooms, but no occupants. Some of the beds were covered in animal print satin sheets, in one room the toilet was left unflushed. It looked as if these rooms did hold someone recently and they were cleared out in a hurry. She was about to give up and move on to the floor below, when she found one door locked. Catalina jiggled the handle and pushed on the door, but it did not open.

"Campbell!" she called out, banging on the door. A couple of seconds later, there was a faint knock back. Catalina banged twice in response, stood off to the side, and fired at the door handle. She then rammed into the door hard with her shoulder. The door gave and swung open.

29

The eerie, but welcoming, quiet was suddenly interrupted by a strange banging sound. Campbell's body tensed. The sound repeated. His eyes flew open, his senses on full alert. Bang. He crawled on the floor to the door, listening. Another bang. The sounds were coming in rather equal intervals. And it sounded like slamming doors. Campbell knew his room was not the only one on the floor, the entire floor was lined with rooms just like his. He was able to figure it out as he was being dragged to and from his torture sessions. What he did not know was whether the rooms were occupied or if he was the only resident. Another door banged. Then everything went quiet before erupting in clapping sounds of gunfire.

His insides jumped with hope that he was being rescued, only to be crushed with a reminder that it was probably yet another sadistic show put on by Chen to torture him. He crouched by the door listening. But this time, he was sure that the sounds were not coming from the speakers hidden in the ceiling of this room. He was certain there was something going on in the hall outside his door. The gunfire stopped, picked up, then stopped again. There was a pattern—someone was shooting at someone else. And whoever was returning fire seemed to be much better at it. After a brief silence, the banging on the doors continued.

The bangs were getting louder and moving toward his room. And closer together in intervals—someone was moving faster. When he distinctly heard the door of the room next to him bang open, he jumped up from the floor. But nothing happened. He stood plastered to the wall, listening. And then someone tried to open the door to his room.

"Campbell!" he heard someone call out banging on the door. Only he could not respond, his door was padded. All he could manage was to knock as hard as possible on a small metal casing around the door jam. Someone banged twice in response. Campbell leaned back on the wall, relief suddenly flooding his entire body. He heard shots being fired at the door and then it was rammed open.

The figure that broke through was not what he expected. It was clad in black tactical gear, heavily armed, yet moving rather gracefully. The room and the hall were poorly lit, he could not make out a face.

"You're a hard man to find, Agent Campbell," said the figure with a hint of amusement. With shock, he instantly recognized the voice. Catalina Bennett.

"You're dead! This isn't real!" Campbell said in disbelief.

"And Hello to you too! Alive and well, thank you very much," Catalina responded and pulled on his arm. "Come on, we've got to get you out of here." She pulled him out of the room toward the stairwell.

Still in shock from Catalina's rise from the dead and weak from all the torture and the fried chicken diet, Campbell was moving rather slow and wobbly. Catalina grabbed his arm and started pulling him along. Just as they were about to approach the door to the stairwell, she heard loud footsteps. Chen's reinforcements had arrived. Catalina pulled Campbell down to the floor and ordered him behind the round purple velvet couch. Before he could protest, or ask for a weapon of his own, she armed herself with MAC-11's and met the incoming assault from the stairwell with rapid and deafening fire. No one stood a chance. She simply tossed aside the now spent machine pistols before casually walking over to Campbell and yanking him up back to his feet. 'Yep, she's alive and well,' confirmed stunned Campbell to himself.

They made their way through the dead bodies into the stairwell. Catalina started to descend, Campbell reluctantly followed.

"He's got one more floor. That's the easiest way out," she explained.

"Give me a gun," asked Campbell.

"No. Just duck when I tell you," retorted Catalina.

The floor they were about to enter was not the last one Chen-the-Chin owned. But it was the only one with an elevator that connected Chen's lair with the downstairs lobby. Catalina's exit plan was to take the elevator, throw on a trenchcoat she brought with her on the ride down, and simply walk out the front door right past the enormous sculpture of red cherries gracing the lobby. But a quick assessment of Campbell's appearance told her that slipping past the foyer guard unnoticed might not be as easy: he was wearing a dirty t-shirt, black combat pants, and a pair of Chinese canvas slippers. Chen must have taken his boots when he stripped him of all his gear.

Catalina gently pushed the stairwell door open and carefully peeked out. The floor they were about to enter was even more gaudy than the one they just left. Large crystal chandeliers hung from a mirrored ceiling, and all walls were covered with tasteless paintings in metallic paint. Catalina spotted a bank of elevators about 50 feet to the left. She figured that behind every column lining the hall someone was hiding with a gun—she would just have to shoot her way to the elevators. And she would have to give Campbell a gun so he could cover her back. Reluctantly, she reached into her bag, pulled out a Beretta

M9, and handed it to Campbell without saying a word. He nodded and took the weapon.

They exited the safety of the stairwell back to back: Catalina facing left, Campbell right. Almost immediately they were met with fire. Their return fire was a lot more precise: they quickly dispensed with their opposition and made their way to the elevators. Catalina pushed the 'down' button, and leaned on the wall to catch her breath.

"I'm out," said Campbell showing her his empty Beretta.

"You might not need it anymore, but Ok," replied Catalina. She was about to reach into her bag to get him a fresh magazine, when something way down the hall caught her eye. She turned to get a better look. Campbell noticed how her whole body suddenly tensed up. He looked down the same direction she was and froze. Chen-the-Chin.

30

Catalina could see him down the mirrored hall, aimlessly spinning in his giant motorized wheelchair around a bright-lit room at the end, screaming for his men. But no one came, there was no one left alive. He was a sitting duck and he knew it. Catalina looked at Campbell, then back down the hall.

"Come on, let's go!" Campbell urged. "This place will be swarming with more guns, or worse—Chinese cops, any minute. Do you want to be caught?" Catalina reloaded in response. "Some targets are just not worth it," he said quietly.

She cocked her head slightly to the side, and Campbell realized that she was listening to an earpiece. She looked down the hall again, narrowing her eyes slightly, then suddenly shoved Campbell behind a mirrored column. *"Uno momento!"* she said. Catalina drew her Glocks and began firing into still spinning Chen-the-Chin, while moving down the hall closer and closer. By the time she reached the room, her magazines were empty and the chair stopped moving. She reloaded, the empty magazines bouncing off the black marble floor as they ejected. Catalina pushed the chair with her foot so Chen faced her. His head was slumped down onto his chest, blood was everywhere. Catalina looked him over slowly, then holstered her guns. She was about to check for pulse, but then pulled her hand back—Chen was so fat, she doubted she would be even able to find an artery. Campbell, pissed for being shoved behind a column, yanked a M16 from under one of the dead bodies left in their wake and slowly moved behind her in case she would need cover. He reached the brightly-lit room just as Catalina pulled her arm away from Chen. Campbell thought she was done, when Catalina stepped behind the wheelchair. She yanked Chen's head back by the greasy hair, and—in one swift yet smooth motion—sliced his throat. She wiped the blood off her knife on Chen's shoulder before sliding it back into her pants.

"Whoa!" exclaimed Campbell. "That's a little excessive!"

"Had to be sure he was dead," she answered calmly. She then whispered something in Italian into her wrist, Campbell realized she was confirming the kill. Catalina pulled out her earpiece and let it dangle on her shoulder while looking around the room. The room was shiny white top to bottom, and lit extremely brightly by large overhead lights. The back wall was covered with banks of servers, all blinking with little blue lights, and labeled in Chinese. She looked at the servers from top to bottom, pulling out a couple of drawers. Campbell missed her slipping something out of her pocket and plugging it inside one of the server drawers. "We should destroy this," Catalina said finally.

"Yeah, good idea," agreed Campbell. "Look around, see if there is a control console, maybe he's got a self-destruct."

"I have some explosives, but they're back down the hall," said Catalina, looking around for a something resembling a tablet or a computer.

"Maybe it's on his chair," wondered Campbell. He walked slowly all the way around, but could not find anything. Catalina walked over. "I saw an iPad once… he used it to film me," Campbell remembered. He also remembered the torture that followed and shuddered slightly. The shudder did not go unnoticed by Catalina.

"Maybe he swallowed it," she said, trying to lighten the mood. She pulled out her knife and used the tip to move around the large folds of the silk robes Chen-the-Chin was encased in. "There!" she tugged on Campbell's arm to get his attention.

The iPad was wedged deep between Chen's enormous gut and the chair.

"I do a lot of questionable things, but I am not touching that! I'm going to get the bombs," Catalina said with disgust, and headed down the hall.

Her bag of toys was right where she dropped it, Catalina knelt down to look for her state-of-the-art explosives. They looked like hockey pucks and her bag was full of them. Suddenly, she saw Campbell running toward her with Chen's iPad in hand.

"We've got company coming!" Campbell thrust the tablet in her face. Catalina quickly scanned what appeared to be live feed from multiple CCTV cameras. She noticed that the rooftop feed was still on a bypass loop she established earlier. The rest showed heavily-armed men moving in. 'So that's how you got captured—you were overrun!' realized Catalina suddenly in her head.

"Yeah, we gotta go," she confirmed, not willing to tempt fate. "I can't take that many." The cocky statement made Campbell raise an eyebrow. Catalina rummaged in her bag, then zipped it shut, and hurled it down the hall toward Chen's room as hard as she could. She pulled Campbell to follow her in the opposite direction.

"The rooftop is the only clear option," he urged her.

"That feed is fake," she said, rushing down the hall, careful not to trip over any bodies. Her right hand was skimming the mirrored wall up and down as if searching for something. "I came in through the roof."

"What are you looking for?" asked Campbell, noticing her hand moving on the wall.

"He's got a… Found it!" Catalina's fingers ran up and down along a thin vertical mirrored panel until she came upon what she was looking for. She pressed something with her index finger. The mirrored panels suddenly slid open revealing an elevator, covered in more purple velvet and wide enough for Chen's wheelchair.

She shoved Campbell into the elevator before entering herself. "This better be a fast one," Catalina mumbled, eagerly pushing the 'down' button. The elevator closed, jerked, and suddenly hurled down. The doors opened into a concrete hallway just as the entire building shook from a sudden explosion.

"Oh, shit! You're going to bring down the whole building!" Campbell suddenly realized that Catalina set the charges on all of the explosives she had in her bag. She simply shrugged and shoved him out of the elevator.

The concrete hallway led to the lower level of the garage. The vast space was mostly empty except for several large vans that must have been used to move Chen around. Catalina was about to break into one of the vans when she saw it. A bright red monster of a vehicle—the armored, mine-protected Marauder. 'So he does have it!' thought Catalina, as she ran up to it. The Marauder was tightly squeezed between concrete columns and blocked by large wooden crates in the front, but she was able to open the passenger door. She whistled at Campbell to get his attention. He ran over and stopped dead in the tracks when he saw what she was planning on driving out of this place.

"You've got to be kidding!" he exclaimed.

"Get in!" she urged instead. He shrugged and climbed up. 'This I've got to see!' he thought.

Catalina was feeling around below the dashboard so

she could hotwire the vehicle. Campbell looked at her for a bit, then calmly reached above her head and lowered the visor. A set of keys fell into Catalina's lap, barely missing hitting her on the head. She gave Campbell a dirty look and started the monster.

"You're blocked in," Campbell stated calmly.

"Not a problem." Catalina reversed roughly, then shifted gears and plowed forward. The Marauder simply crashed through the crates, just as more explosions ripped through the building overhead. As they were about to make it out of the garage, their path was suddenly blocked by two black SUVs—Chen's reinforcements. Catalina hit the gas and rammed right into them, pushing them aside as if they were made out of cardboard. The red brick street, tightly lined with parked cars on both sides, was too narrow for the Marauder to drive through. But Catalina made a sharp turn and simply gunned it down the middle, leaving a long trail of crumpled cars in her wake.

It did not take them long to reach their destination— an abandoned lot in the seedy part of Hong Kong, surrounded by piles of garbage and a rusted chain-link fence. Their trail was clearly marked by the massive amount of cars the Marauder punched through. Catalina parked right in the middle of the lot. 'A bright red monster sitting fully exposed in this neighborhood… We're toast!' thought Jim. He was about to ask her what they were doing here, when she turned to him and said:

"I'm sorry." Before he could react, she jabbed a large injection pen into his thigh. Pain and heat shot instantly through the tissue, spreading fast. He passed out.

31

New York

McCarthy never wanted to go back to work, but Marina persuaded him. She swapped his phone for a burner, kissed him on the cheek, and reminded him that his allegiances were no longer with 'God and Country'.

"Yes, dear!" replied McCarthy. Marina pushed him out the door.

For the past 48 hours, McCarthy did nothing but pace up and down in their living room, wearing out the hardwood floors and nagging Marina if she heard anything. She got so annoyed with him, although understanding of his state of mind, that she sequestered herself in the kitchen downstairs keeping busy with new recipe development. The Company finally started to inquire into McCarthy's absence and whereabouts, and he was forced with the decision of either resigning or going back in. The Family needed him back in. Marina supplied him with a doctor's note about a nasty viral bug and sent him on his merry way.

If there was one thing McCarthy was great at—it was keeping up appearances. As he stepped off the elevator, he was once again the distraught and worried agent whose partner and friend was in distress. He checked in with everyone for a status update—there was none—and even stormed into Peel's office demanding action just as soon as the man walked in. McCarthy watched Peel slam his keys on his desk, and noticed a little plastic keychain. It could have been a USB drive, but it was very small—almost a little square. McCarthy pressured Peel for answers on Campbell's status, now just to misdirect him from the fact that he noticed Peel's keychain. Peel gave him the same story of having his hands tied, but just as McCarthy was about to leave, added that the matter was now handled by the State Department. Which struck McCarthy as odd—why would State be handling something that was not supposed to be on the books anyway? The way Peel acted when he said it was also odd—he fidgeted, his eyes darting from side to side to avoid looking directly at McCarthy. Peel had a tell, McCarthy suddenly realized. And, he was lying.

McCarthy sat at his desk, his suitcoat hanging on the back of his chair, blankly staring at his computer screen. In his head, he was replaying all the conversations he previously had with Peel. He closed his eyes, trying to visualize Peel's behavior, looking for a tell he just picked up on. If Peel was lying now, he had to be lying before as well. McCarthy was mentally sorting through months-worth of conversations, when the phone Marina gave him vibrated in his pocket. He checked text messages—there was only one. It was from Marina's number. The text simply said: <all done.> Campbell was rescued. McCarthy let out a huge sigh of relief. As he was pocketing his phone, the floor was suddenly flooded with reports of a building exploding in Hong Kong. One Island East. Chen-the-Chin's building. McCarthy grabbed his suitcoat and rushed out. His disappearance went unnoticed in all the commotion.

32

Provincia di Palermo, Sicily

Jim woke up with a start and bolted upright. He was confused, the surroundings were unfamiliar to him. He rubbed his face and looked around. The room looked like a hotel suite—a large king-size bed with white luxurious linens and lots of pillows, white décor with ostrich leather, exotic lacquered wood, and highly polished intricate brass fittings. The room was dim—heavy curtains covered one entire wall. Jim stumbled out of bed in search of a bathroom. He found it right by the door across from a large closet. The bathroom was appointed with floor to ceiling slabs of Carrara marble. The towels were crisp white and extremely plush. A shaving kit and a new toothbrush were set out by the sink on a white paper mat. The little designer shampoo bottles reaffirmed his suspicion that he was in a hotel.

He took his time showering, the multiple body jets invited him to linger with his eyes closed, washing away the grime of his captivity along with the fried chicken scent that seemed to have penetrated deep into his skin. In the closet he found a pair of jeans and a t-shirt, but no underwear or shoes. He just shrugged it off and got dressed.

Jim tried the door, but found it locked from the outside. Momentary panic washed over him, he crossed the room in large strides, snapped open the curtains—and came face to face with a muscular guard armed to the teeth. Only a piece of large glass that formed the sliding door separated them. The guard, who was slowly chewing on something, looked Jim over and then slid the door open. Jim did not move. The guard made a motion with his rifle, which Jim identified as a Sicilian Lupara, and then pointed in the direction of a stone path that ran right by the glass door. Jim slowly stepped outside and was instantly hit by the warm fragrant air. He squinted against the bright sun and started down the path.

His eyes were darting from side to side, trying to take in as much of the surroundings as possible. Citrus trees lined the path on both sides, providing large pools of cool shade. Big men lounged in the citrus shade, either smoking or chewing on a toothpick. All heavily armed. 'Someone's private army,' thought Jim and wondered whose prisoner was he now. He could see an outline of a modern villa down the path. As Jim walked by, the armed men stopped their chewing and smoking to slowly look him over. Their glances were cold, and a bit hostile. He would nod to the older ones as a sign of respect and ignore the young. There were a couple of chuckles behind his back as he passed, but no conversations.

The citrus trees gave way to luscious palms and bright tropical foliage. He noticed a large infinity pool, big enough to swim laps in, and a vast loggia that seemed to wrap around the villa. The villa was clad in white stucco and had a traditional red clay tile roof. The top of the roof was littered with satellite dishes and large antennas, indicating that this was no ordinary house. Jim stopped at the end of the path to look around. There was someone swimming in the pool, but he could not see who it was. His view was blocked by a gentleman in his 50's, impeccably dressed and holding a folded white plush towel in one hand and a small silver tray with an umbrella drink in the other. 'Butler!' thought Jim. He had never met one before.

Someone tapped Jim on the shoulder. He turned. His room guard was standing behind him, still chewing on something. He stopped his chewing to say something to Jim that sounded like Italian, only Jim did not understand a word of it. The guard pointed to the villa. "All right, all right!" Jim said and slightly raised his arms in surrender, before starting toward the loggia. The guard stayed on the path, watching him. Out of the corner of his eye, Jim noticed that the butler never took his attention away from the pool.

It was much cooler under the roof of the loggia. The ceiling was vaulted and bedecked in some exotic wood Jim could not identify. Large modern fans slowly rotated, lazily pushing the air around. The low wicker sofas were large, with clean straight lines and overstuffed white Sumbrella cushions. A square Carrara marble coffee table sat between the sofas. This was not just high-end outdoor furniture, this was bespoke. Jim slowly moved inside the villa, through a tinted accordion glass wall which could open up completely and disappear. Today was the perfect day to do just that—the wall was partly folded to create a wide opening.

The room Jim walked into was a dining room. His feet, burned by the hot patio stones outside, welcomed the coolness of the terrazzo flooring. The dining room was dominated by a long mahogany table surrounded by black Wishbone chairs. Jim recognized the chairs right away, he once considered them for his loft until he saw the price tag. This dining room had 20. Not one, but two black Murano glass chandeliers hung above the table. A nice collection of Degas pastels in gilded frames hung on the wall above a long buffet cabinet.

It seemed that there was no one around. The villa was eerily quiet. Jim looked around wondering where to go next. There were two closed louvered doors on the right, and a wide opening leading into other living areas to the left. He chose left.

The dining room connected to a large long space with high vaulted ceilings. The space was divided by furniture into several conversation zones. All the outer walls were tinted glass and opened outside to the covered loggias. Soft Turkish rugs covered the terrazzo and helped divide the space. The furniture was deep, low to the ground, and upholstered in white linen. A well curated collection of art hung on the mahogany-panelled wall opposite the windows. The space was well designed and luxurious. But, just like his loft, it felt brand new. Unlived in. Cold.

He continued to move though the living area, until he came upon the front entrance. He could see a small courtyard outside with an antique marble fountain and long garage with multiple glass doors. To the right of the entrance was a small bathroom and a steel door. He tried the door and discovered that it was locked.

Beyond the small bath was a large open kitchen with a butler's pantry that led into both dining and living rooms. The kitchen was outfitted with sleek Boffi cabinets and all the latest culinary gadgets. A massive La Cornue range in cobalt blue, and a matching hood above, dominated the middle of the kitchen. Whoever lived in this house was serious about food. And polished brass—the trim on the range was so shiny, Jim's eyes were beginning to hurt. He noticed that both ovens were on, something was cooking, but he decided against peeking inside. A small marble-topped bistro table with two rattan chairs stood by the large open doors that led outside to a small patio surrounded by a vegetable garden and citrus trees. A louvered door by the stove led Jim back into the dining room.

There was still not a soul inside, he could see the butler standing at attention by the pool. Jim moved toward the other louvered door and tried the handle. It gave. He slowly pushed the door open with his finger and peaked inside. He was looking at a library.

Unlike the rest of the villa, this space felt somewhat lived in. Books filled the shelves to the ceiling, framed paintings were leaning against each other on the floor. He recognized a couple of Renoirs and a Gauguin. Two wooden crates, designed to hold a painting, stood in the corner. The curtains were partly closed, a massive TV built into the bookshelves on one wall was turned on but muted. Someone liked watching BBC News. He noticed another door across the TV, it was slightly ajar. *Vogue Italia* and a Sotheby's catalog lay open on the couch. But what took his breath away was a large round Hermès leather tray sitting on top of a tufted round ottoman. The tray was overflowing with Fabergé eggs. He had never seen a collection like this all in one place. And sitting out in the open, not under a lock and key. He reached out to touch one, but jerked his hand away at the last moment. He felt like the eggs had sordid stories, ones that would never be told.

"You can pick one up if you like. They don't bite," he suddenly heard behind him. He spun around. Catalina was standing in the door, dripping wet, wrapped in a white fluffy towel, and holding the same umbrella drink he saw the butler hold earlier. So it was her swimming in the pool.

"Hi," was all that Jim managed.

"*Ciao!*" she responded with amusement and leaned on the door jam. The butler appeared behind her. "We'll need something to eat," she said to the butler without turning her head. "Inside."

"*Sí, Signora,*" replied the butler and disappeared into the kitchen. Catalina moved into the library and set her drink on the small side table next to the couch. Water was dripping from her long hair, she was leaving small puddles as she moved.

"You're gonna need to tell Butler what size shoes you wear, he dared not to guess," she said to Jim as she pushed the other door wide open. Her massive bedroom was behind the door. Jim followed her in. "I could tell him what size you wear," she continued, "but then he would know." She smiled and gave him a wink as she moved across the room—referring to their rendezvous on his rooftop in New York.

"This is your house..." Jim said absently, looking around the room. Her massive bed was still unmade, a silk nightgown was pooled on the bench at the foot of the bed. Something stirred inside him.

"*Sí*. You're in my villa," Catalina replied quietly.

"What time is it?" he asked.

"Early enough to still have breakfast… Or it can wait," she responded and leaned against the wall. Suddenly, he crossed the room in large strides and pulled her toward him. She instantly responded. Her towel was tossed on the floor, his t-shirt followed. They never made it to the bed.

In the kitchen, Fernando the butler brewed himself an espresso and sat down to relax with a thick book. He never bothered to start on breakfast, and figured it would at least a couple of hours before they would ask for lunch.

33

They missed lunch. At some point, an order came from the bedroom to dismiss the *decina* for the remainder of the day. Fernando gave it lip service and instead told Catalina's soldiers to scatter but remain on premises. He did not trust Campbell and felt better knowing there was well-armed muscle around. Plus, Catalina's men followed *Omerta*—the Mafia code of silence—they would never disclose to anyone who their Capo was sleeping with.

Antonia showed up with groceries, and left almost immediately rather embarrassed and mumbling about not stocking the bedroom with condoms. Fernando occupied his sudden free time by ordering a suitable wardrobe for Campbell, he sized him up in the couple of minutes he saw him, footwear included. He chose briefs over boxers, chuckling to himself 'When in Rome, wear what the Romans do!' He used Don Carlo's tailor, fully aware that the details of the order would make it back to Don Carlo almost immediately. It was his way of keeping the Don in the loop without compromising his position with Catalina.

Dinner time came and went. Fernando made up a large tray with a mountain of sandwiches, pastries, and fruit and left it by the bedroom door along with a bottle of wine. Ferruccio stopped by to see if there was anything new to report back to Don Carlo. He raised a curious eyebrow when he heard that there was nothing new. A while later, Frank called to check in as well. Fernando told him the same thing he told Ferruccio: "Those two have not come out of the bedroom since morning." Which made

Frank very grumpy. "Quite the stamina he's got," Frank commented. "Chen must've not tortured him enough."

Hours later, Fernando heard the shower running. He took the opportunity to check and see if the tray with food has been picked up. It had, and it was returned. Empty. He brought the empty tray back into the kitchen and turned in for the evening.

Catalina and Jim finally emerged three days later around tea time to take a dip in the pool. Catalina found Jim a pair of swim trunks; she kept a variety of swimwear in the villa in case her family visited. The swim trunks were European in style, extremely small and snug. Jim looked uncomfortable and exposed, Catalina could not stop laughing at his predicament. From his perch in the kitchen Fernando could hear her laughing and was enjoying her happiness, however fleeting that might be. He served them English high tea on the loggia, and was dismissed for the day shortly after.

"What's your butler's name?" asked Jim, while helping himself to a cucumber sandwich.

"To you—Butler," answered Catalina. She poured Jim a cup of Earl Grey and placed it in front of him.

"What am I supposed to call him? Butler? I can't believe you even have a butler."

"You will not call him anything, he works for me. And why not? Plus, he was hired by my grandfather, I didn't have a say in the matter," Catalina said with a slight shrug. "He really works for him, but I don't have a problem with that. Nonno likes to keep tabs."

"Nonno, you mean the Don?" asked Jim. The agent in him could not let this one slide.

"Yes, the Don. *Capofamiglia*. The Boss. The Head of the Family… Also happens to be my grandfather. A rather nice likable guy, actually," Catalina retorted. "He's retired, he won't kill you. At least I think he won't." Jim got the point.

"We need to talk about what happened. In Hong Kong, I mean," he was not the type to ever discuss what happened in bed, especially when it felt so right.

"We will, but not yet. I don't have any intel for you yet, why stress over nothing? We put the feelers out, when we catch something I'll let you know and we'll take it from there. There is nothing to do now. Just relax, have some tea." She put a couple of sandwiches on her plate, and reclined back into the sofa.

Jim took the dainty teacup in his hand. The smell of bergamot reminded him of home, yet somehow he felt at home on this loggia, next to Catalina. The feeling was confusing to him. He decided to just enjoy this moment for now.

They ate their cucumber and smoked salmon sandwiches in silence, enjoying the rustling of citrus trees in the gentle breeze and the shimmer of the pool. Suddenly, Catalina declared that she wanted to go dancing. Jim was surprised.

"Come on, my cousins have a really swanky club in Palermo, we'll just drive down there. It's a lovely drive up the coast, you'll love it," she pressed.

"I've seen you drive, I doubt it."

"I'm an excellent driver! There are some fun cars in the garage. Come on!" Catalina was being very persuasive.

"I have nothing to wear!" It was his last excuse.

"Nope, you can't use that one! A—you're a man, B—I'm sure Butler took care of it by now. Let's go see what you got!" she jumped off the sofa, pulling him up to follow her. He took his teacup with him.

34

She did not make him wait. In fact, she was waiting for him. Jim found Catalina in the living room, looking at something on an iPad while lounging on one of the white linen couches. She was wearing a white shift dress covered in large beaded petals resembling waterdrops. The dress was a boatneck with little cap sleeves made out of the waterdrop petals. It was extremely short, exposing Catalina's mile-long legs in all their perfectly tanned and toned glory. She wore strappy white and gold stiletto sandals with unmistakable red soles. Long, intricately crafted, gold and precious stones earrings dripped from her ears—besides the diamond Cartier Trinity ring she always wore, the earrings were her only accessory. Catalina put away the iPad and got off the couch when she saw Jim walk in. Her body moved confidently and fluidly, despite the dangerously high heels. She slowly looked Jim over—starting at his Gucci-clad feet, then slowly moving up to take in the whole look of perfectly-tailored light gray suit and a white shirt he left open at the neck. Jim unbuttoned his suit coat and struck a pose.

"Nice!" she smiled with a chuckle.

"Your butler has impeccable taste," remarked Jim.

"Butler didn't put this together, Don Carlo's tailor did," she corrected, gathering up her gold clutch and large dark shades framed out with little pink flowers. "It's bespoke, we did not have time to outfit you in Tom Ford," she dropped as a matter of fact and started walking toward the front door. Jim, wondering exactly how Catalina knew about his Tom Ford preference in suiting, followed behind her.

Catalina exchanged words with a large mustached man standing guard by the front door. The man rested his rifle next to the door and disappeared.

"I asked him to clear the driveway, I want to take one from the garage," explained Catalina.

"You've got a Ferrari in the driveway," commented Jim.

"Ah, it's just a Ferrari," she shrugged with indifference. Jim wondered what could be more interesting than a red Ferrari 458 Spider. He followed her into the garage through the steel door he noticed when he explored the villa three days earlier.

Catalina's garage was state-of-the-art and clean as a whistle. Tool chests lined the walls, framed vintage race flags for various Italian race teams hung above them. The concrete floor was so shiny and clean, one could eat off of it. It was a five bay garage, all full. Some of the cars were carefully covered. Jim made out the shape of an Aston Martin under one of the covers. This garage was a car aficionado's paradise, except for a large gun case hanging on the wall by the door into the villa.

Catalina walked all the way to the end, and pulled off the cover on the last car. The Alfa Romeo Disco Volante. 'Yep, much better,' thought Jim. He had read about the hand-crafted piece of automotive art, but had never seen one up close.

"Cool, huh?" inquired Catalina. She opened the glass garage door and the Alfa's nose glistened in the sunshine. Jim walked slowly around the car, gently running his hand along the meticulously sculpted red curves.

"They paint it gold first to get this color," he remarked quietly, almost to himself. Catalina stood off to the side, watching him admire the car. She made the right choice. Jim knew cars, a Ferrari would not have been as gratifying as the Disco Volante.

"Does it really sound the way they say it does?' he asked.

"Oh yeah… Come on," answered Catalina and got in. Jim was about to experience the throaty savage roar of the Alfa on the open road. But, as a passenger. Catalina was driving.

They took the SS113 along the coast to Palermo. Catalina usually zipped in and out of traffic at high speeds, but today she felt like cruising. Jim leaned back in his red and black bucket seat and closed his eyes. Catalina did not turn on the stereo—she loved the sound of the Alfa's engine. Jim's CIA-trained brain kept wondering about the Family's finances, how exactly they acquired all these exotic—and rare—cars. He knew there was a vintage Ferrari 250 GTO in Catalina's garage, he noticed that the black Audi R8—identical to the one she drove in New York—was swapped for a lime-green Lamborghini by a short fat man earlier in the afternoon. At first he was going to ask Catalina what that was all about but realized she would just blow him off. The Lamborghini did not stick around to Jim's relief, it disappeared a couple of hours later. He found the lime-green iridescent paint hideous.

They rolled into Palermo and made their way north to a popular neighborhood filled with bars and clubs. Catalina turned into a narrow quiet alley surrounded on both sides with centuries-old buildings. Bus boys lazily kicked around a football, waiters in long white aprons leaned against the stone walls smoking before the start of their busy shift. Everyone scattered to let the car slowly pass through. Catalina waved hello. Someone let out a long slow whistle at the car in adoration. The Alfa stopped in front of a steel door, simply labeled 'trattoria'.

"Where are we?" inquired Jim.

"This is my cousins' place. There's a dance club upstairs. But first, we eat," answered Catalina and got out of the car. Jim followed.

"Front door's not good enough?" he asked after looking up and down the alley. The bus boys resumed their football game, trying not to get the ball anywhere near the Disco Volante.

"I don't eat in the dining room," explained Catalina. Jim opened the heavy door for her, then followed her in. The door led straight into a large restaurant kitchen, with meal preparations in full swing. "I get the best seat in the house, Chef's table."

A tall, thin, dark haired, young man in Chef's whites rushed over to greet them. His face had similar features as Catalina's and his eyes were the same color, only much warmer and friendlier. He exchanged the customary hello kisses with Catalina; then shook Jim's hand while sizing him up with suspicion. He introduced himself as Giacomo, Catalina's cousin, and guided them to a small table in the middle of the large kitchen. The table was set with white tablecloth, placesettings of modern design, and so many wine glasses that Jim lost count. He helped Catalina to her chair, then sat down himself. Catalina explained that there were no menus, this was Chef's choice and Giacomo loved to show off, especially in front of her. Jim silently prayed that Don Carlo's tailor was a generous man and his pants had room to grow.

35

New York

McCarthy tailed Peel home. He had an unsettling feeling in the pit of his stomach about the man. And Campbell taught him to listen to his gut. McCarthy shared his uneasy feeling with Marina—she calmly suggested that he should sit on Peel for a couple of days to see if anything strange happens.

Peel was an easy target to follow, he never checked his tail. He lived right off Central Park, and McCarthy wondered how he could afford such an address. Marina showed up in an older model non-descript Chevy that she parked up the street from the building. McCarthy was about to inquire as to how she got the car, but decided against it. He got into the car, she gave up the driver seat, but failed to send Marina home. She brought a picnic basket and a plaid thermos filled with espresso. When McCarthy asked—half joking—where was he supposed to relieve himself, Marina handed him an empty orange juice container without saying a word. He got the feeling this was not her first stake-out.

They waited for hours. With the picnic all gone, the car was starting to fill up with the stale odor of food. Marina sensed that Nick was not in the mood for chit-chat, so she entertained herself with her phone. He was about to give up for the evening, when suddenly Peel came out and flagged a cab. Marina jumped out of the Chevy, leaving Nick alone to tail the cab. She watched him fall in behind the cab, then turned toward Peel's building. Marina pulled down the V-neck of her shirt to reveal even more cleavage, pushed her boobs together, refreshed herself with a liberal dose of Dolce&Gabbana Light Blue to cover up the stale food smell, and sashayed into the lobby. Five minutes later, the doorman escorted her upstairs to Peel's apartment.

"He won't return for a while, but don't take too long anyway," instructed the doorman and left her alone. Marina waited for the door to close, then looked around to get her bearings. Peel lived in a small one bedroom pre-war apartment. "Rent-controlled," figured Marina. She headed into the kitchen first. She related to people through food, the contents of one's fridge spoke volumes to her. Peel's kitchen had not been remodeled since the 80's. There was a dirty coffee spoon stuck to the Formica counter next to a Keurig coffee machine. Marina took a tissue out of her Gucci bag and used it to open the fridge. She did not want to leave any prints.

The fridge contained a half empty carton of store brand orange juice, a carton of expired eggs, and several Chinese takeout containers. A nearly empty bottle of Russian Standard vodka and a small premade pizza were the only occupants of the freezer. Marina rolled her eyes. She photographed the contents of the refrigerator and then proceeded to open every cabinet with the same tissue. She found lots of paper plates, bare minimum in cookware, and a large drawer filled with delivery menus. She carefully looked through them using a pen she found in her Gucci bag and took several pictures.

Satisfied with the kitchen, Marina moved to the living room. She worked quickly through the room—there was not much of interest there. The bathroom, also stuck in the 80's with an oak vanity and an octagonal maroon sink, could benefit from a decent scrubbing and lots of bleach. Peel's toiletries were generic, except for a bottle of

Jean Paul Gaultier Le Male cologne, and he washed his face with a bar of soap. Marina snapped more photos and moved to the bedroom.

"Uh, snooze fest," remarked Marina. She quickly looked through the closet and a small chest of drawers, peeked under the bed and behind the lonely framed art, and was about to leave disappointed when she spotted a small photo album on the bottom shelf of the night-stand. 'Nobody uses a photo album anymore, hmm…' she thought and bent over to take a look.

"Bingo!" exclaimed Marina after carefully opening the cover. The album contained room keycards from hotels around the world. She made quick business of flipping through the pages and snapping photos of every card, then replaced the album and beelined out of the apartment. On the way out of the lobby, she thanked the doorman by slip-ping him a hundred dollar bill with a handshake.

"I barely found it," she lied to the man with an exag-gerated sign of relief, patting her Gucci as if it contained her precious find.

"I'm glad you did. Stay away from that one, he's a fuck-ing asshole," cautioned the doorman. Marina nodded in agreement and hurried out of the building.

McCarthy found Marina in her work kitchen. It was just her and Mike, cooking up a storm. The sounds of Latin music from Mike's iPod were being drowned out by the overwhelming noise of mixers, blenders, and siz-zling sounds from the salamander broiler. Marina, sway-ing to the beat, was pulverizing something bright green in a commercial blender. Nick carefully walked over and tapped her on the shoulder. He startled her, she jumped. He motioned to her that they needed to talk, but she scooped out a spoonful of the green mystery sauce from the blender and shoved it in his mouth.

"What is it?" yelled Nick.

"Aioli. I'm playing around with new flavors. Good?"

"Yes, only I don't know what an aioli is. We need to talk!"

"Yes! We do! Hold on a sec!" Marina poured the bright green contents of the blender into a square container, covered it with plastic, and motioned Nick to leave. On the way out, she checked on something in the oven. "Yo, Mikey! You're burning!" she yelled to her sous chef. Mike stopped his chopping and rushed to rescue the dish.

"What are you cooking in there? Sounds like the two of you are waging a war on produce," Nick could not help but comment.

"Oh, a bit of this, a bit of that. Just testing some recipes we came up with," vaguely answered Marina, her hands saying a lot more than her words. Nick knew that she cooked as an emotional relief—she was trying to hide her anxiety.

"This late in the evening?"

"Well, we started this afternoon. Mike's got a day off tomorrow anyway… What'd you find out about Peel?"

"I tailed him all the way to Chinatown," answered Nick. He moved into their kitchen to make Marina a cup of green tea. Decaf. "He went into a restaurant whose name I can't pronounce. I decided not to follow him in."

"The restaurant, was the name in Chinese? Like four characters?" asked Marina, eyes narrowing.

"Yeah, how do you know that?" asked Nick.

"Well..." Marina went into the library and returned with a massive pile of color printouts. She dumped them on the island counter and started sorting. "Like this?" she asked, thrusting a photo printout of Chinese food containers inside a fridge.

"Yes! Where did you get is?" Nick demanded to know, getting a rather sinking feeling.

"I bribed the doorman and got into his apartment," explained Marina calmly. As if bribery and breaking-and-entering were normal things to do. Which—in her world—they were totally normal things to do, realized Nick. He let it go, he was impressed with her operating skills.

"His fridge was full of these. Unless he gorges himself, I'd say a week's worth of leftovers," continued Marina.

"What else did you find?"

"Well, the apartment is rent-controlled. Trust me, I know." Marina organized her printouts before continuing. "He's cheap, drinks a lot, knows his booze, can't boil water, needs a whole new wardrobe, definitely packing but I don't know what, should clean his bathroom once in a while, and shops duty free. The doorman called him a 'fucking asshole' I'd take his word for it." Every characteristic was backed up by a printout of photos she took, placed on the counter with a rhythmic snap of her wrist. She ignored the cup of green tea Nick placed next to her. "But that's nothin'..." said Marina and paused.

"What?"

"He travels. A lot," said Marina with smug satisfaction. Triumphantly, she placed in front of Nick the large pile of photos she took of all the hotel keycards.

"Wow!" Nick uttered in awe. He paged through the pile. "Where did you get this?"

"He has them all in a photo album next to his bed. Be careful, they're in the same order he had them. It might be chronological, some of these look rather dated."

"He doesn't travel that much for the Company, he's not in the field... Oh, this is good. Really good!" Nick pulled Marina close, tilted her chin up to face him, and planted a kiss on her lips. "Between this and the Chinese joint, we'll find something. I *knew* he was fishy!"

Marina took a photo of the takeout food from the counter. "Let me ask Mike about the restaurant," she said.

"Mike? Your sous chef?" asked Nick confused.

"Mike knows every single joint in New York, he's better than Zagat. Did you really think I only kept him around for his knife skills?" Marina folded the printout and headed downstairs.

Nick flipped through the printouts of the keycards, absently drinking Marina's green tea. He was itching to pop over to the office to see what, if anything, the Company had on these locations. But he knew that he could not. Not without raising a red flag and drawing attention to himself. Downstairs the noise from the mixers had gone quiet. Nick's thoughts turned to Marina's comment on Peel being cheap, he found it out of character with the persona Peel projected at the work with the massive redecorating of his office. 'Who are you?' thought Nick. Marina returned, carrying a large silver tray heavily laden with food. Dinner.

"That restaurant is a front. Chinese Triad owns it. Food sucks, but the back room gambling is top notch," she delivered while unloading the tray on the dinner table. "Mike warned to stay as far away from that joint as possible. Said they're able to run a background check on the spot and know who you are as soon as you open the door."

"Interesting. What kind of gambling, does he know?" inquired Nick. He got out the utensils and walked over to the table.

"Anything and everything. Horses, sports, poker. Some Chinese game," answered Marina sitting down.

"What Chinese game?" asked Nick, taking the seat across her.

"Pai Gow? What is it?" she answered with a shrug.

"Chinese dominos."

36

Provincia di Palermo, Sicily

At some point during Catalina and Jim's meal, Giacomo pulled up a chair and joined them. He inquired whether they were having a good time—Catalina raved about his gorgonzola panna cotta. He eagerly explained the elaborate process involved in making this amazing cloud-like morsel, only Jim was completely lost after the word 'enzyme'. He changed the topic by complimenting a different dish. Giacomo nodded happily, then complained like a spoiled child about the quality of an ingredient to Catalina.

"Call my father," she suggested. "He seems to have a finger on the unobtainable."

"I'd rather come down there and see him," said Giacomo. "Last time I came, he treated me to those langoustines of his. Bastard wouldn't reveal his source!"

"Of course he wouldn't. He just wanted to see you beg," explained Catalina, then put down her fork slowly. "And don't you ever call my father a bastard in front of me," she stated coolly.

"*Mamma mia*, I'm so sorry, I won't! Never again! So sorry!" apologized Giacomo quickly. Jim noticed how Giacomo's expression and body language suddenly changed, as if he was a child being scolded by his parent. Jim deduced that, even though Catalina and Giacomo were cousins, she was a lot higher up the organizational ladder than he was. Jim wondered just how high.

"Visit my father tomorrow," Catalina said to Giacomo changing her tone slightly. "He's been rather bored lately, he could use a little distraction. Your problem should occupy him for a while." Giacomo agreed, then quickly excused himself back to his pots and pans.

On the ride back, Jim decided to prod a little about Giacomo: "He's afraid of you, isn't he?"

"He should be. I'm made, he's not. Never will be. My father's a made member too, Giacomo should show more respect," answered Catalina matter-of-factly. But Jim sensed there was a lot more to it.

They never made it to the dance floor. After finishing their elaborate and delicious meal, Catalina did not like her cousin's choice of the night's DJ. But, they still got to dance. Back at her villa, Catalina had an elaborate sound system with a turntable. She put on a record as soon as they got back from Palermo. She turned up the volume, flooding the entire villa with music. Tango. Catalina was in the mood for tango. And Jim was more than happy to oblige. He learned to tango while being on assignment in Argentina—his assignment was boring and required little effort, so he killed his abundant free time by taking dance classes. He figured dancing would come in handy one day, but Missy could not put one foot in front of the other and they never danced. When Catalina first brought up dancing, tango was the first thing that crossed Jim's mind. He figured it was a long shot, however, since they were going to a popular dance club. When he heard the first couple of notes of the record Catalina put on, he was surprised and elated. Tango suited her—elegant, seductive, sensual... Masterful... Just like her. They danced Tango Argentino, tightly embraced, under the Sicilian night sky by the pool. He was good, she was better. She confessed at one point that both her parents were quite the dancers and she was taught at an early age. She showed him a few new moves. He lead her right into the bedroom.

Catalina sat up in bed, wide awake. She looked over her shoulder at Jim, he was sound asleep. The twisted sheet barely covered his lower half, his naked muscled chest rising slowly with each breath. Catalina bit her lip in temptation, but forced herself out of bed. She slipped on a long silk robe, quietly tiptoed out of the room, and made her way down to the living room. Her hand slowly ran along the highly-polished mahogany wood wall, her palm finding the all too familiar spot. She stopped and spread her hand over the wood, a faint blue line suddenly moved up and down her palm. Biometric scan. There was a little pop, and a large wall panel cracked open. Catalina pushed the panel in and slid inside the room it revealed. She pushed the door back with her bare foot, failing to close it completely.

The dimly lit room was her lair. The room contained enough ammunition and weaponry to outfit a small army, screens and server panels lined one wall. Two PixelSense tables dominated the floorspace in the middle of this square windowless space. The room sat at the core of the villa, in fact the villa was built around it. It was a bomb shelter, a weapons storage, Catalina's op center, and a death trap for anyone who was not invited.

She plopped into her Aeron chair, leaned back, and put her feet up on one of her PixelSense tables. She usually slept the sleep of the dead, no matter what the situation was, so when something kept her awake—she paid attention. Something nagged at her, it was the reason why she woke up. Something she picked up on a while back and just filed away in her mind. She needed to sift through her memory in order to retrieve the nagging thought, and she could not do it with Agent Campbell sprawled naked on her bed. She closed her eyes and took a deep breath.

It was something recent. Something still fresh. She was on a job... Just last year... Japan? No. Monaco? No, that just turned out to be a set up hit for Nunzio's boys. The Irish? Nope, definitely not the Irish… And then it hit her—Karlovy Vary. That strange clumsy exchange with the Frenchman. Catalina flung her feet off the table and sat up in the chair. The entire memory came clearly into view. Suddenly, a quiet but high-pitched shrill filled the room. Someone, whose biometrics were not coded into the system was approaching the entrance. Catalina swiped her hand across the PixelSense table to view the CCTV feed. The living room cameras, tiny and concealed in the ceiling, revealed that Jim was up and about. Catalina rolled her eyes and got up to intercept him.

37

Jim, sleeping, turned to his right side and lazily reached for Catalina. His hand found nothing but cool sheets. He ran his hand up and down her side of the bed, then opened one eye. She was gone.

He rose up slowly, and looked around. "Babe?" he called out. There was no answer. He untangled his legs from the sheets and got out of bed. Jim stumbled to the bathroom, completely naked, but Catalina was not there either. He looked around for something to cover himself up with and settled on a pair of pants still crumbled on the floor by the foot of the bed from last night. He pulled them on and left the bedroom in search of Catalina.

A couple of early mornings he woke up to use the bathroom only to find that Catalina was not in bed. Every time he was about to go searching for her around the house, he heard Butler moving about. Catalina always returned a couple of hours later, just in time for breakfast. She smelled of dust, sun, and propellant. Jim would pretend to be asleep—he rather enjoyed the unique way she woke him up.

He first checked in the kitchen, but no one was there. He then checked out the dining room, peeking outside to check out the pool. Nobody. Jim padded slowly into the living room, the floor cool on his feet. Seeing that Catalina was not in the living room, he was about to leave when he noticed a sliver of bluish glow spilling from a crack in the mahogany wall. 'So there is something in the middle,' confirmed Jim to himself. After days of carefully investigating the villa, he realized that the square footage of the rooms did not exactly add up to the outside dimensions of the villa, suggesting that there must be a concealed space somewhere. Only he failed to find it.

He moved toward the sliver of bluish light. It looked like one of the wall panels was open, leading to somewhere. Jim got closer, when suddenly the panel swung open and Catalina emerged. She put her hand on the wall, the panel slid closed behind her.

"Did I just find your Batcave?" inquired Jim.

"If I tell you, I'd have to kill you," she was serious. Jim dropped it. She was entitled to her secrets.

"I couldn't find you. Are you OK?"

"Couldn't sleep. Which is rather rare, I have to say." Catalina started walking toward the kitchen. Jim followed.

"Something on your mind?"

"Yeah. Come on, I need a nightcap." She flipped on the electric teakettle and started rummaging through the fridge. Jim brought over the prosciutto ham, resting on its stand on one of the counters. Catalina pulled out various cheeses, a large jar of green olives, and juicy tiny red tomatoes still firmly attached to a deep green vine. Jim pulled out an aromatic loaf of bread from the bread box. They filled a platter with slices of prosciutto, cheeses, a bowl of olives, and tomatoes. The kettle dinged. Jim brewed a pot of teasan, Catalina's nighttime favorite.

She suggested they sit outside by the pool, Jim instantly agreed. The night air was crisp and fragrant, the dark sky peppered with shiny stars. The pool, lit from within, provided ambient light. The water was still, like glass, shining in the moonlight. They loaded all their food, along with a fat English teapot full of tea, on a large silver serving tray. Jim was about to carry the tray out, when Catalina covered the teapot with a brightly colored crochet tea cozy.

Jim raised an eyebrow in silent question.

"Little old Sicilian widows. They wanted to make sure your tea stayed hot," explained Catalina.

"My tea? How do they know I like tea?"

"Honey, by this point the whole island knows you like tea," dropped Catalina in response and turned on her heel.

Steam was slowly rising off the surface of the pool, it was still being heated in case they decided to take a dip. Catalina lit the candles inside the enormous lanterns scattered around the loggia. Jim placed the heavy tray on the Carrara marble coffee table and they got comfortable on the wicker sofas, wrapping themselves with sapphire blue cashmere blankets. He looked out over the pool into the deep shadows of the citrus trees and caught little orange dots glowing here and there—Catalina's men having a smoke while patrolling the property. He realized that they were never alone, there was always someone watching from shadows.

Catalina caught Jim staring out into the trees. She followed his gaze and picked up on the flickering orange dots. Her eyes narrowing in displeasure, she suddenly whistled and made a gesture across her neck. The orange dots disappeared.

"*Idiota!*" said Catalina with disgust.

"Not allowed to smoke, huh?" inquired Jim.

"Some of my soldiers are slow in kicking the habit, unfortunately," explained Catalina. "Even though it's hazardous to their health in more ways than one. The glow gives up their position, they can easily be picked off one by one," she said as a matter of fact, then leaned toward the food tray and took a slice of cheese. Jim was startled at how her brain worked: he simply noted that they were not alone, but she noted that the men were easy targets.

"The kid that's been hanging around," said Jim after

taking a long piece of prosciutto.

"Ferruccio. What about him?"

"He's got potential. It would've been nice to develop him."

"Oh no you don't! He's mine, I'm developing him," stated Catalina.

"What is he, a cousin?" asked Jim out of curiosity.

"No. He started out working in my Nonno's kitchen, but we all quickly noticed that he has potential. A lot of it."

"Did he know whose employment he was entering? What if he wanted to just be a chef or something like that?"

"Oh, he knew. His grandfather worked for us, his widow—Ferruccio's grandmother—still sends salamis for the Don's table… He needs to go to college though. Somewhere out of your reach, of course."

"Well… I'm still pondering how on earth did the Company miss you?" wondered Jim.

"They didn't miss, I just hid very well. I knew what you guys look for, my father clued me in, and did the exact opposite. I learned from his experience not to work for anyone with three-letter ID's. Plus, I was already working, so I wasn't on campus a lot."

"Working… Oh geez!" Jim caught on what work she was referring to. He knew this was as far as this conversation was going to go, and decided to change the subject. The less he knew about her past, the longer he lived. "So, what woke you up tonight?"

"We'll have to wait on the brie, it's not soft yet," pointed out Catalina. Jim popped an olive into his mouth and poured her a cup of teasan. She put one leg up on the sofa and leaned back. "There was something I saw, not so long ago," she started. She took a thin and long piece of prosciutto, tilted her head slightly, and slowly lowered it into her mouth. Jim found the maneuver quite provocative, but contained himself. If she was willing to talk, he was going to listen.

"It was an exchange, or at least an attempt at an exchange. It was so clumsy, no trade craft," continued Catalina. "Something like this stays with you, you know?"

"Yeah, I know the feeling. You don't know what you saw, but you know something's off."

"So you just file it away, until one day it suddenly becomes clear." Catalina took a sip of her tea. Jim rolled a piece of prosciutto around a slice of hard cheese, Catalina raised an eyebrow. He offered her a bite, she waved it off and reached for an olive instead.

"Suit yourself," shrugged Jim. "I like the way this tastes."

Between ribbons of prosciutto and bites of bread slathered with softening brie, Catalina filled him in on the details of the sloppy exchange she witnessed in Karlovy Vary. Jim listened without interrupting, noticing that she was only giving a general description of the people involved.

"You're right, sloppy," he commented when she was finished.

"I told you. I usually don't care about other people's business, but this was strange. In our line of work, things that are a little odd, or out of place, stand out the most. Raise the red flags." Catalina lifted her teacup, slowly bringing it to her lips. Jim could not help but nod in agreement.

"So… which one was your mark?" asked Jim point blank. The teacup stopped just short of her lips. Catalina's eyes narrowed, the teacup was slowly lowered back on its saucer. Jim looked straight at her, waiting.

"The Frog. I took him out on Christmas, he proved a rather difficult person to get close to," she finally answered.

"The Frog… Frenchman… On Christmas…" There was something familiar about a killing in France during Christmas. Paris. He remembered going through the French papers Peel requested. "Oh Jesus! You slit his throat!" realized Jim.

"Yep. Give the client what they want, right?" she finally took a sip of her tea. Jim decided not to push further. There was no need to know who paid for the hit.

They continued to polish off the platter, when suddenly Jim sat up in his chair. "The other man in Karlovy Vary, what did he look like?"

Catalina gave Jim a long and detailed description. She saw in his eyes his mind was racing, processing each detail. Suddenly he slammed his fist on the Carrara marble coffee table. The dishes rattled.

"You know him don't you?" asked Catalina quietly. Calmly.

"Yes! That son of a bitch!" snapped Jim. "It's Peel! He's my boss!"

38

New York

How does one break into his own workplace after hours? His unlisted, CIA workplace? And does it without being noticed? McCarthy was pondering this question all night long. His plan was to just come back into the office after hours and pray to God that no one would notice his presence. Over a dinner of mushroom and cheese ravioli, Marina came up with a much better idea. Her plan was to dress Nick up as a janitor in order to sneak back into the office and not get caught.

"No one ever pays attention to the help," she explained. "You walk in with the cleaning crew, do whatever you need to do, get out."

"And how exactly am I going to do that? All the janitors have IDs," inquired Nick. He had to admit though, her idea did sound good.

"Easy. This is New York. You're in a commercial building. Janitors have to be union. And unions is something I know about. I've got a guy. Don't worry."

She supplied him with a uniform, an ID—fake of course—and a contact in less than a day. Late in the evening, right before the cleaning crew was about to start their shift, he was met by a wiry stubble-faced guy by the back entrance to his building. McCarthy caught a glimpse of a prison tattoo on the guy's neck. They did not exchange words, just nodded in recognition. McCarthy was instructed earlier to follow his contact's lead—the guy was to get McCarthy to his own floor and watch his back. The guy got him through security check-in and gave him a cleaning cart. They rode up to McCarthy's floor in a freight elevator. On the way up, he was given a silent crash course in office cleaning so he could pass as a janitor on surveillance cameras.

Peel's office was unlocked. McCarthy—wearing a uniform of gray shirt and pants, an old baseball hat to cover his face, and a white dust rag stuck in his back pocket—rolled his cleaning cart to the door and walked inside. He was armed with an enormous feather duster, and thought he looked utterly ridiculous when he caught a reflection of himself in Peel's glass wall. McCarthy walked over to Peel's desk, carelessly running the duster along the surface to move some dust around. The desk had five drawers. Two on either side: small and big, and one in the middle for a keyboard. The left big one contained files—nothing unusual or classified—and a half empty bottle of whiskey. The right one was empty—this is where Peel kept his briefcase. The left small drawer contained some toiletries and a clean shirt in a plastic bag—also not unusual since long days were part of the job description. The right side held a massive amount of pens and pencils, tangled together in cords from old computer mice.

McCarthy carefully went through all the items, wearing rubber gloves intended for cleaning toilets. He did not find anything interesting. Not a note, or a recording pen, or an unauthorized cell phone. McCarthy sat down in Peel's chair and turned on his computer. It was not hard to guess Peel's password, he was not very creative. McCarthy went through his files, and noticed that Peel's clearance was high enough to access the personnel files of all the NOC agents. He poked around some more, but could not figure out if anything was copied. Frustrated and upset, he returned the desktop to the way he found it, then shut it off. McCarthy pushed in the keyboard drawer and was about to get up when he saw something.

A little plastic case slid from under the keyboard. He picked it up to take a closer look. It was small and made of clear plastic. He had seen cases like this before—micro SD cards were usually stored in a case like this. McCarthy lifted the keyboard to see if the card was lodged under there as well. No card. But the empty case was still a good solid lead. He remembered he noticed a USB key chain on Peel's keys, perhaps it was a micro SD card reader. All he needed to do was to track down the missing SD card.

Filled with the possibility of taking down Peel, McCarthy energetically jumped off the chair. He ran the feather duster across the desk, tempted to knock over the Koon's balloon rabbit, and grabbed Peel's trash can to empty it out. As he was dumping the trash into a large bin on his cleaning cart, his ex-con companion motioned to him to wrap it up. McCarthy nodded and returned the trash can back under Peel's desk. The case for the micro SD card was safely inside the deep pockets of his janitorial pants.

McCarthy's companion offered to escort him out of the building, he was not going to make him clean the toilets. As they rode the elevator down, he suddenly spoke: "all that stuff in that office—expensive. But no taste. They call it art—it's not art. It's ugly, not even worth stealing. Give me a nice little Degas any day, now that's art. Guy must be a real putz to own that Koon rabbit!" McCarthy could not contain himself and broke out in laughter. The ex-con—a recovering art thief and a forger—chuckled along.

39

Provincia di Palermo, Sicily

The cat was out of the bag. Jim now had a target, someone to chase. Catalina could not contain him. He asked for a phone and a computer—he wanted to get in touch with McCarthy. Both requests were gently, but firmly, denied. But McCarthy was able to pass, through Mark, everything he had learned about Peel so far. Including his theory that whatever Peel stole was put on a micro SD card. Mark sent McCarthy's intel to Luciano, who in turn passed it on to Don Carlo. Don Carlo ordered it to be delivered to Catalina, without even looking at it. Helping one CIA agent hunt down another was something he had no interest in. He did allow Catalina the use of the Family's resources if she needed more intel. "One less rat," he said. "Make sure he puts him down," Don Carlo ordered Catalina.

Not willing to let Jim into her Op room to use her technology, Catalina forced him to piece everything together the old way—pen and paper, and messages sent to various underworld contacts. Ferruccio did a lot of running between Catalina and Luciano, who was willing to make the necessary calls to speed things up.

One day over lunch by the pool, Catalina told Jim about finding a micro SD card inside the Frenchman's safe, and that it was labeled *Chen*. Jim immediately wanted to get his hands on that card. He needed it to prove that Peel was dirty. But Catalina could not understand why he wanted to spend all the energy and resources on chasing down an item that might no longer exist. It would be a lot easier to just track down and kill Peel.

"Proof," explained Jim. "I need proof. I can't kill someone without a reason. I don't work that way."

"You kill people for the Company on orders," retorted Catalina.

"No I don't. I'm not a mechanic. I'm just an operative," Jim quietly said.

"So when you give the order," continued Catalina with a shrug of indifference, "do you explain to your mechanic why he's pulling the trigger?"

"Actually, I do. I always read them in," answered Jim, leaning in and resting his elbows on his knees.

"You must be the only one then."

"Probably…"

"Well then…" Catalina put on her dark Gucci sunglasses and got up from the table. She gave him a look—he saw her jaw tighten even though he could not see her eyes through the shades—then turned on her heel and walked away.

Jim leaned back in his chair, pondering if the card indeed still existed. He wanted it, needed it, so he could be sure that Peel sold CIA secrets. He also wanted to go back to work. All this lounging around was starting to get to him. Deep down he knew that Catalina would be more than willing to put him to work, all he had to do was ask. But joining the Mafia was never in his career plan. 'I just need to nail this son of a bitch,' he kept telling himself.

Jim was antsy. And messy. Catalina liked to keep everything in tidy little piles, labeled, and in sequence. Jim's work was a total mess. Printouts and handwritten notes followed him everywhere. Once, a pile of papers blew into the pool and had to be fished out. Fernando tried to keep up with Jim's mess, but eventually threw his hands up in defeat and announced to Catalina that he would clean up after Campbell left, hinting that he should leave sooner rather than later. Catalina herself finally broke down and left Jim alone one afternoon to visit Nonno.

She found Nonno in his newly-remodeled dining room, about to have lunch. He invited her to join him. She liked the new décor of the room—it was brighter, paired-down, and more modern. The large dining table still dominated the space, but the walls were stripped of their gilded wallpaper and painted custom-blend white. The heavy and dusty drapes blocking all the windows were gone as well. The antique sideboards were replaced by one massive modern piece. And finally, there were enough matching chairs for the entire family. Along with a couple of extras hidden away in the cellar, in case Nunzio planned to continue his chair-breaking habit. The lunch was simple Sicilian seasonal fare, and they ate in silence.

"What am I doing?" suddenly asked Catalina. She stopped and looked at Nonno, waiting for answer. They moved to the garden to take a leisurely stroll in hopes of walking off their lunch.

"Sowing your oats? Sometimes we have to do irrational things, to get them out of our system," suggested Nonno, absently chewing on a toothpick.

"Is that how you ended up with so many children? All from different women?"

"No, that was because I did not do the irrational thing. I played it safe. Many times over, yes, but safe. The women I loved were not my enemy." His eyes glazed over with memories of the many women he loved. And left behind.

"I can't believe I'm doing this. Why can't I just let him go?" Catalina kicked a piece of gravel with her foot in frustration. "What the hell am I doing?" Nonno did not answer and he continued to walk forward, the toothpick moving up and down between his lips.

"Take him to the Field," said Nonno suddenly. He stopped and turned to face Catalina. He pulled the toothpick out of his mouth and briefly examined the chewed end. "Show him who we are. Show him that we will never change, and that our business will always be murder. Then, you'll know." He placed the toothpick back into his mouth and continued walking.

40

The next day, Catalina drove Jim out to the Field before lunch. "I want to show you something," was all she said. She parked under a lush olive tree to keep the Merc in the shade. She walked out toward a large grassy area, Jim followed.

"We call this The Field... This is where we train... From a very early age... We've owned this land for generations, locals avoid it. They say it's full of ghosts. They're right," explained Catalina. Jim looked around the large overgrown field, potmarked with various size holes and small mounds. There were rows of targets set up at various distances.

"Ghosts? You must have some bodies buried in here then," he tried to lighten the suddenly dark mood. He sensed that there must be a reason she was showing this place to him.

"Of course. But they're from way before my time," Catalina explained, deadly serious. "My cousins have a map, so they don't accidentally blow up any graves when they test their handwork. I've never seen it though."

She was walking toward a series of targets set up way back at the edge of the field. She was looking straight ahead, yet walking in an odd serpentine pattern. Instead of following her footsteps, Jim started walking straight, when suddenly his foot twisted on a small divot in the dirt that he failed to notice. He realized that Catalina's strange pattern was to avoid all the holes and bumps in the ground, and that she knew every square inch of this field by heart. He rubbed his ankle, then followed her steps precisely all the way to the targets at the edge of the Field. Catalina stopped when she reached them and waited for Jim to catch up to her.

"Who's practicing?" asked Jim. The targets were large metal sheets that hung off wooden posts, with human silhouettes painted with black paint.

"Me." Catalina had a strange look on her face as she slowly traced with her long finger the rough hole her round made in the metal target. She looked like she was dreaming of something.

"The Field's almost 2,000 yards," Catalina said quietly. "I've been practicing for a long time… yet, it still eludes me… Perhaps it's best left for the next Benedetto." She shrugged and walked away.

Jim walked around to see the target Catalina was examining. It was riddled with holes, none—however—hit the mark. 2,000 yards… 'Shit!' Jim realized Catalina had been practicing a 2,000 yard shot, yet kept missing. Without comprehending, he breathed a sigh of relief. Jim missed that Catalina was watching for his reaction. Her dark Ray Bans hid her gaze turning cold at his obvious sigh of relief, he missed that she straightened her back and took a slight step away from him. Coming to the Field, showing him the practice targets, all this was a test—and Jim blew it. Someone who valued her skill—an equal—would be eager to discuss the details of her challenge, but an enemy would be relieved at a sign of weakness. She turned on her heel and started walking toward the car. Jim followed. Suddenly she stopped and turned to face him.

"Peel. He's the source of all your troubles, I'm sure. Wanna get him?" she asked, her tone was cold and all business.

"Yes!" Jim answered immediately.

"Ok. We traced Chen's courier. The trail leads to Moscow. We start there."

Slowly rocking in his old chair under the cool cover of his loggia, Frank watched the Merc drive off through a rifle scope he used instead of binoculars. Next to his chair, covered by an old tarp, stood Catalina's target from her last practice shoot. Last night Frank ordered Ferruccio to switch it out with the old one—he knew that she was going to walk Campbell through the Field. The target had several holes—all of them hit their mark dead on. Just as Frank predicted—with Ferruccio being her spotter, Catalina finally hit the 2,000 yards.

———

Brooklyn Heights, New York

"Who are you?" Mark asked his computer. The computer did not respond. He had been combing through the data dump Catalina initiated on Chen's servers before blowing them up. The data was incomplete due to the explosion, but still extremely interesting. A couple of Russian aliases peeked Mark's curiosity. He was able to connect those aliases to the Frenchman, together with what McCarthy provided he tied them to the SD card Campbell was looking for. Only the faces that went with the names were not Russian at all and their legends had rather thin 'window dressings.' He had just gotten word that his sister was on her way to Moscow. Now more than ever, Mark wanted to peak behind the 'curtain' to give Catalina as much intel as possible.

"Who the hell are you?" Mark asked again, and cocked his head a little. The screen did not respond. "Well, let's see if someone can find out who you really are. Because you ain't Russian!" He moved to a different computer and was about to enter a chat room, when there was a knock on the door. Suddenly, a little cherub waddled into the room. Sofia, Mark's daughter. She was followed by an old Jewish man with a warm wrinkly face and a gaze that did not miss a thing. He was panting a little from helping the chubby toddler up several flights of stairs.

"Hi Ari!" said Mark to the old man, after taking his daughter into his arms. "Are you feeling all right?"

"Yeah, yeah, I'll be fine." Ari rubbed his chest and sat down on the couch.

"Why don't you let me install an elevator in the building?" asked Mark. Still holding Sofia, he sat next to Ari on the couch.

"Nah. Why bother? It'll only attract attention. And inspectors. Once you leave, we'll move to Boca," answered Ari, eyeing the boxes in the corner. He also noticed the multiple computer screens—Mark was working. "Why don't I take Sofia to get a treat from Ruth? Come over when you're done. Come on, Sofia! Let's see what Bubbe Ruth has in store for you today!" He got himself off the couch and extended his hand to the toddler. Sofia wriggled out of her father's arms and trotted to the front door. Ari snuck a peak at the screens, and followed Sofia. Mark returned to work. He caught Ari sneaking a peak at what he was up to, but was not bothered by it. Catalina's longtime New York landlord, and a Holocaust survivor, vowed a long time ago to take Benedetto secrets to the grave. Catalina rewarded his friendship and loyalty by handsomely providing for retirement in Boca Raton, whenever he and his wife Ruth decide to finally move down there.

Mark carefully crafted his inquiry on a piece of paper before entering a Dark Web chatroom. He spent some time saying hello to his various hacker friends, even helping with a line of code here or there. He communicated carefully, staying away from anyone eager to discuss recent high profile hacks or anything that made the headlines. He knew that cyber cops patrolled the same chatrooms and he did not want to get on their radar. Mark strategically singled out a couple of people that could potentially help him with his query. Finally, after several long hours, he nonchalantly posted his question. <Heck if I know, but it's time we find out, right?> was one of the responses. <Let me get back to you,> was another. No one signed off, which was a good sign that his inquiry did not make anyone suspicious. He burned his piece of paper over the sink, then ground the ashes in the food disposer. Now all he had to do was wait and see what his colleagues came back with. Mark decided it was a great time to take a break and pick up Sofia from the Abramovitzes.

Late at night, Mark checked in on his inquiry and found that it bore fruit. There were several responses and lots of attached encrypted files. It would take hours to decrypt everything and piece it all together. He needed caffeine. Mark found a box of chocolate-covered coffee beans in the kitchen, afraid that his fancy European espresso maker would wake up Sofia. He popped a handful of beans in his mouth, wiped the hand on his pajama pants, and got to work.

"Oh shit!" exclaimed Mark suddenly after several hours. He stared at a file he just finished decrypting. The Russians were not Russian at all: they were Chechen mob. He scrambled to find his satellite phone. "Pick up, pick up, pick up," he whispered as the phone started to ring on the other end. Mark crossed his fingers hoping that the new intel would reach Catalina in time.

41

Provincia di Palermo, Sicily

They met in Don Carlo's kitchen. Ferruccio was perched on a wicker stool by the corner of the massive butcherblock waiting for her. One of the widows, buzzing around the kitchen in a colorful apron tied around her traditional black dress, asked him if he was hungry. He politely declined, yet a plate of steaming spaghetti with fragrant tomato sauce appeared in front of him anyway. The sauce tasted like summer in a jar. When Catalina appeared, the widows quickly and quietly left the kitchen. They knew she was here on business, and it was not food related.

For the past several hours, Catalina had been organizing a trip to Moscow for herself and Campbell. At some point, Frank called and suggested she arrange a backup as well. She agreed. Catalina slipped out of the house under the guise of picking up Campbell's new legend. She explained that her cobbler was skittish and she had to come alone. Campbell did not question her—this was her turf. Ferruccio, who had been staying away from her villa ever since Campbell took notice of him, met Catalina at Don Carlo's.

"I need you to go to Vienna," said Catalina, after laying out her Moscow plans to Ferruccio in great detail. "I have a Sanctuary all set up there, it's very well equipped. You'll be able to track us from there. Vienna is centrally located and you've been there before so you can operate there with no problems. Moscow is complicated. We'll save that lesson for another time."

"Not a problem," nodded Ferruccio.

"Once we're out, you can get closer," continued Catalina.

"I got you. Close, but not too close for him to notice."

"Precisely." To Catalina's pleasure, Ferruccio was a quick study.

She gave him directions to her Vienna Sanctuary, a shipping container outfitted to her particular needs and stashed out of sight of authorities in a Family controlled location. Ferruccio committed the directions to memory and took off to arrange his passage to Vienna. Catalina stopped by Nonno's office to say goodbye, only to discover that he was not home. Nonno's butler Inch suggested that perhaps Catalina could stop by a bit later.

"We're all loaded up, I've got to take off in an hour," replied Catalina.

"I'll tell Don Benedetto that you stopped by. *Buon Viaggio!*" said Inch. He insisted Catalina take Don Carlo's silver Morgan Aero Coupe in exchange for the Alfa Romeo Disco Volante she drove up in. She took the Morgan, yet left the estate with an uneasy feeling in the pit of her stomach.

The sleek Gulfstream G650 glistened under the hangar's bright overhead lights. The metallic jade green Mercedes G63 pulled up right next to the plane. A young man in dark blue overalls ran up to the car and opened the door for Catalina. Jim was left to open his own door. The young man quickly unloaded their luggage from the trunk, then jumped into the car and pulled it away. A white Range Rover was parked by the tail, several armed men were loading heavy metal crates into the plane. Catalina told Jim to board and went over to talk to the men. With Catalina's Merc now parked in the back of the hangar, the young man was back loading their luggage into the plane.

There was speed and efficiency to everyone's movements, noted Jim. They had done this many times before. The pilots were already in the cockpit. Besides the pilots, there was only one other crewmember—Fernando the Butler. He was the steward on this flight. Jim was surprised to see him but did not show it. He simply deduced that Catalina preferred to run a small crew with several people filling multiple positions. What Jim did not know was that Fernando was the mastermind behind their Moscow legends. He was not only Catalina's butler, but her personal cobbler. He traveled with her when possible and used the time to establish the backstops needed for her elaborate fake backgrounds. He was one of Catalina's trade secrets that she would never share with anyone.

Jim could not help but notice his surroundings. She had a nice plane, decked out in white Italian leather and ebony wood with black and white plaid carpet. There was a small aft bedroom, also in black and white. The air smelled of citrus and leather polish. The plane was bought second-hand from Eddie, the Benedettos stripped it and had it redone to their own specifications. Their redesign objectives were style and smuggling capabilities—they had achieved both.

By the time Jim seated himself in a large leather chair and took a glass of champagne Fernando insisted on, Catalina boarded. She signaled the pilots to take off and sat down across from Jim. Fernando immediately appeared with her champagne flute and a crystal bowl of fruit. Jim swiveled his seat around so he could face her.

"Nice plane. Very Chanel," he commented.

"Don Carlo's a longtime fan of the brand. Don't spill anything," said Catalina, as she watched how Jim held his champagne glass. He noticed her pursed lips and carefully put the glass down on a cocktail napkin. "And don't bother memorizing the tail number because it's fake. Nothing is real off the island. We work really hard at keeping it that way," she warned. Jim said nothing. She nailed it: the tail number was the first thing he looked for when he saw the plane.

"You always drink champagne when you're heading out on a mission?" he inquired.

"We're off to Russia, pretending to be spoiled super rich brats on a party circuit. Gotta have garbage to match. Trust me, they snoop through everything. I even had Butler collect empty bottles from the family so our consumption rate matched our stories," explained Catalina. She took a sip of her champagne and offered the fruit bowl to Jim. The plane taxied to the runway.

"Is that what those metal crates are? Decoy garbage?"

"Nope. Unlocked iPhones. A crate of iPhones greases a lot of palms in Russia. I brought two."

"iPhones… Good call! We usually bring cash and then worry about the bag the entire flight," commented Jim. Catalina just rolled her eyes.

The pilot announced to prepare for takeoff. Jim swiveled his seat back into its original position. Fernando disappeared toward the back. Catalina took another sip and got comfortable in her seat. 'Moscow. This better be worth it,' she thought as the plane took off.

42

Moscow, Russia

About three hours later, they landed in Moscow. They waited inside the plane for the customs official, whom Fernando greeted warmly with a fat envelope and a casual mention of the crates filled with iPhones. The official quickly dispensed with the travel documents, then welcomed everyone to beautiful Mother Russia and gave them his personal cell phone number in case they needed anything. A black Mercedes-Benz S class was already waiting for them when they disembarked.

The drive to Moscow from the airport took almost as long as their flight. The traffic was horrendous, driving was dangerous. The driver, a huge middle-aged man in a black leather jacket and a very expensive Omega watch, kept a suspicious eye on Jim in the rear view mirror. From the driver's brief exchange with Catalina when they got into the car, Jim deduced that the two must have worked together before. He wondered how far did the Family connections actually spread. The driver warned Catalina, in heavily accented yet fluent English, that every car was now outfitted with a camera since there were a lot staged accidents to extort money out of drivers. Catalina asked if he knew how to disengage the camera. He did, and provided her with instructions. They were stuck in non-moving traffic at that point. Suddenly, a drunken bum appeared out of nowhere and splayed himself over the hood of the Mercedes. "I'm hit, I'm hit," he moaned. "You hit me! Call the police!" The driver colorfully told the drunk that the car was outfitted with a camera that recorded him climbing on top of the hood. The drunk refused to get off. Catalina calmly ordered the driver to deal with the situation. He got out of the car and dragged the drunken scum off his vehicle. Jim could not see what happened next. The driver appeared a minute later. He brushed off his gloves before getting back in the car. "See? This is why we need camera!" pointed out the driver. It was another half hour before the traffic started moving again. The drunk never returned.

Catalina and Jim were dropped off at the Ritz Carlton on Ulitsa Tverskaya. The luxury hotel was located across the Bolshoi Theater and a short walk away from the Kremlin and Red Square. Catalina slipped the driver his generous cash payment, adding that there was a little extra in the envelope for his unique problem solving skills. He unloaded their suitcases into the porters' capable hands, while Catalina and Jim went to check in.

The opulent hotel was breathtaking. The lobby was filled with beautiful women in the latest couture and men in bespoke suits. Catalina pouted and whined a little with every word as she hung on Jim's arm—playing the part of a spoiled jetsetting socialite to perfection. She didn't stop until the valet closed the door of their suite on his way out.

"God, these women are so dumb, it's exhausting! And my face hurts!" she announced, collapsing on the bed.

"Well, that was quite the performance," noted Jim. He walked over to the large window to take in the breathtaking view of the Moscow skyline.

"Enjoy the view, we're not staying here for long," said Catalina. She reached over to the phone and dialed room service. Jim noticed she was flipping through the in-room menu.

"Where are we going?" inquired Jim.

"Somewhere," she said with a wink. She unzipped their suitcases and started unpacking. Jim got what she was doing—creating an illusion that they were indeed staying in the hotel for a while in case someone decided to check them out. He grabbed his toiletries case and headed into the bathroom. When their room service was delivered, he opened the room door in nothing but the hotel bathrobe.

They snuck out of the hotel shortly after finishing off their meal and took the Metro to their final destination: Krylatskoye. Krylatskoye was one of Moscow's districts—*rayon*—located in the Western part of the city, beyond the *Sadovoye Koltso*. It was developed in the mid-80's around the 1980 Summer Olympics Velodrome. The Family had a safe house there in one of the blue and white apartment buildings next to the Metro station. The 17 story U-shaped buildings of Krylatskoye, assembled Lego-style out of pre-fab concrete panels, were far removed from the glitz and glamour of The Ritz. There were kids playing in the large dusty square courtyard created by the facing U buildings, small sedans and SUV's parked tightly along the street. Catalina's flat was on the 14th floor of one of these buildings. It had three rooms with a nice kitchen and a small foyer. The clean-lined décor was dated but the place was spotless and well maintained. The rest of their luggage was already inside when they arrived. There was caviar and fresh food in the fridge and vodka in the freezer.

"Ok, now what?" asked Jim after brewing black tea he found in the kitchen.

"My sources say that Peter Bulanov has your card. Bulanov is your typical Russian oligarch thug, most likely ex-KGB."

"They all are. How did you figure he's our guy?"

"That's what Chen's courier gave us. After Chen's death, his people were more than willing to share. For a price of course."

"That goes without saying." Jim knew he was costing the Benedettos a great deal of money, and he wondered what they expected in return. He did not know that Catalina was personally bankrolling his adventure. When the time came to pay his debts, she would be the only one collecting. "So, how do we get to this Bulanov fellow?"

"Through his son. His youngest son. He's quite the character. Bulanov has two sons—the oldest, Alexander, is the picture of offspring perfection; the youngest, Nicolai, is a bumbling idiot. But the mother loves him. Kolechka, she calls him. Bulanov puts up with him just to keep his wife out of his hair. She knows where the bodies are buried apparently."

"Peter, Alexander, Nicolai… What's the mother's name?" asked Jim.

"Ekaterina. Why?"

"Interesting. They're all named after Russian Royalty… Hmm," explained Jim.

"They're also common Russian names, maybe it's just a coincidence. You can dwell on it later," said Catalina. But a feeling of worry sparked in the pit of her stomach. She willed herself to ignore it and to concentrate on the operation at hand.

"Where do we find this Kolechka?" Jim asked. He offered Catalina some tea, she declined with a slight wave of her hand and went for a bottle of San Pellegrino instead.

"Well, the entire family hangs out at Krysha Mira, the top hot spot in town, however he prefers to moonlight at Marusya. His family has no idea. The website says it's a cabaret for women, so it's safe to say that it's a strip club.

For women. So I get to go and play, you get to sit outside in the car and watch the perimeter." She rolled her eyes. Catalina found strip clubs cheesy and avoided them at all costs. Now she had to go into one on purpose, and in Moscow. She set her expectations as low as possible. Jim could not help but laugh as he saw her face grimace with disgust at what lay ahead.

"I hope you brought singles," said Jim, still laughing. "Or do they dance for iPhones?" Catalina could not help herself and joined him in laughter.

43

Catalina dressed appropriately: a skin tight Hervé Leger black Bandage dress, Christian Louboutin platform stilettos of dangerous heights, lots of bling. The night turned out to be chilly, she threw on a short silver fox fur coat. All the clothes came from a vast wardrobe in the larger bedroom. Jim peaked into the wardrobe and discovered it stuffed with designer clothes, both male and female. The men's clothes were of various sizes, the women's were all one size: Catalina's. She wore a wig of light brown mid-length hair to hide her dark hair, and applied enormous fake lashes and lots of contouring. She looked ridiculous, over the top, and exactly what was expected from a successful modern Moscow woman. She brought a pair of fashionable eyeglasses, with a hidden pin size camera so Jim could have a visual feed, her Apple Watch and Chanel jewelry hid a mic and an earpiece. Catalina told Jim to arm himself, and slipped her Glock 19 into her red leather purse when Jim was not looking. Jim wondered how exactly was she going to be able to handle riding in the Moscow Metro in this getup, but Catalina produced a keyfob to a BMW to settle all his worries. She explained that they only had the car for 24 hours. As usual, the vehicle was hot.

"*Kak tvoi Russki?*" suddenly inquired Jim about the fluency of her Russian. He feared that her accent might give her away.

"*Prekrasno! Slavo Bogu u menia est sluh. A kak tvoi?*" she replied in rapid Russian, rolling her 'r's and without a trace of an accent.

"*Tvoi lutche.*" Jim honestly admitted that her Russian was better than his.

There is Russia, and then there is Moscow. Today's Moscow is glitzy, glamorous, over the top, mystifying, and dangerous. Moscow has three ring roads inside the city limits: the central *Bulvarnoye Koltso* with four lanes of traffic and narrow tree-lined parks dividing the carriage ways; *Sadovoye Koltso* with massive eight, at some points ten, lanes of traffic and no gardens even if it is called the Garden Ring. The third ring was built in the late 90s to connect existing roads with new highways. One could say that *Bulvarnoye Koltso* is the center of glitz and glamour—Russian style—with Bentleys and Porsches parked on every corner, haute couture shopping at GUM, furs and diamonds strolling down the streets, buckets of caviar and rivers of vodka flowing at private parties. Further out, where the majority of Muscovites lived, one could get hit on the head with a hammer for an iPhone. Campbell had not operated in Moscow for over ten years, Catalina pulled on average two jobs a year. She made Jim drive their borrowed black BMW 328d xDrive sedan, after checking to see that there was no video camera mounted on the dash, but navigated his every turn. He dropped her off on *Lesnya Ulitsa*, North-West of *Bulvarnoye Koltso,* and circled around to find a place to park.

The Marusya Club for Women was located on Lesnya Ulitsa in a stone building in the middle of the street. The large Marusya sign, lit in bright white neon, hung above the white double doors. A five foot tall matreshka doll stood on the street, drawing attention to the club. The door was manned by a large, buff, and barely clothed speciman of Russian masculinity. Catalina had no problems passing the face control and was welcomed right in. Jim watched the bouncer give her tight and shapely behind a long and slow once-over as she sashayed past him. He wanted to get out of the car and punch the man in the face, but then they would be blown.

Marusya was a unique establishment. It catered exclusively to women—offering young, hard-bodied, scantily clad men, and a 'Crazy Menu' of services ranging from simple dancing to private rooms. The club was decorated with Soviet military symbols and large flowery prints, all bathed in red light. A dark narrow hallway with rose-patterned carpet and wallpaper and red-shaded wall sconces led to private rooms that contained couches and showers. Russian women came to Marusya with cash-filled designer purses, easily spending thousands a night to be danced with, flirted with, or cuddled with. Or perhaps even something more. Some were looking for a boyfriend experience and had their favorite boytoys, some came for a one night adventure.

Catalina did a discreet comm check with Jim. She had a description of Nicolai Bulanov, but did not know exactly what he did at the club. Her mic was sensitive enough to pick up ambient noise, Jim heard the heavy pounding of bass. She carefully reported her location inside the club, and commented on the abundance of AK47s used as props. She really hoped they were indeed only props. Catalina suffered through several orders of dances until Nicolai finally appeared. Jim was lost for words when he caught a glimpse of Nicolai on the feed from Catalina's eyeglasses.

Nicolai was short in statue, Herculean in build, with dark features and short black hair. He was dressed as a sailor in a striped tank top three sizes too small, tight denim cutoffs that defined his religion, and a white studded leather belt. Nicolai's dark looks raised a red flag with Jim. 'He doesn't look Russian,' he thought. "Order the private room," Jim said to Catalina. "Already done," she quietly replied back. Only it did not go her way. Nicolai refused, extremely politely, and offered to dance and cuddle instead. He explained that he was not working a full shift tonight, and it would be unfair to such a beautiful woman not to have his full attention. Catalina pouted but agreed. And changed her strategy. Very gently, and skillfully, she got him to talk about himself. He spilled that he needed to make a delivery tonight of an item his brother entrusted him with. He patted his overly muscular chest, and Catalina noticed that there was something tubular hanging on a chain around his neck, hiding under his sailor tank. Nicolai was not very bright, and compensated for his lack of intelligence by bragging about his important daily job. Catalina almost had Nicolai wrapped around her finger, when he got a call. He politely excused himself, then exchanged brief, but harsh, words with the caller. Nicolai hung up, reluctantly bid her farewell and left. Catalina discretely followed him to the back of the club and watched him change into street clothes. "He's leaving, pick him up outside!" ordered Catalina to Jim. She quickly settled up her bill with a large wad of cash and rushed outside.

Once on the street, she saw Jim following Nicolai on foot. Nicolai did not get into a car, but instead was walking south down the street. Catalina realized he was walking toward a Metro station. "Shit, he's heading toward the Metro! We have to grab him before he gets there!" she whispered into the comm piece on her wrist as she rushed toward their BMW. She tossed the fur and her purse onto the back seat before slipping behind the wheel. Her extremely high stilettos made it impossible for her to drive, so she kicked them off. The car was facing the wrong direction. Catalina popped the car into gear and decided to just u-turn right on the street. Her maneuver drew

Nicolai's attention and he turned around. The street was barely lit and Jim, not familiar with his surroundings, was unable to make himself disappear in time. He was made. Nicolai paused, then turned back. At first he returned to his previous walking pace, then suddenly bolted.

"Fuck!" exclaimed Jim and took off after him. Catalina hit the gas and followed, intending to cut Nicolai off. Jim noticed Nicolai rip something off his neck and shove his clenched fist into his pocket. "Hey, he's got something on him!" he managed to report to Catalina while in pursuit.

"I know. Just shoot the little shit!' ordered Catalina. Jim pulled his gun and stopped to take aim, but Nicolai ducked down. The surrounding darkness was not helping either.

"I don't have the shot!" reported Jim. Catalina flipped on her brights to help him but Nicolai turned right down another street. Jim followed. Catalina hit the steering wheel with her hands in frustration, shifted gears, and floored the gas. This was not how she pictured this operation going down.

44

The black BMW took a sharp right at full speed, barely missing a bumper of a Bentley, and continued to careen down the poorly lit street.

"No, no, no! Do not swallow it!" Catalina yelled out inside her car when she noticed that Nicolai might have shoved something into his mouth. "Well, you're a dead man now," she commented and hit the gas. Nicolai was fast on his feet, flying down the old narrow street, overcoming obstacles with huge jumps and acrobatic maneuvers. He was fast, but her borrowed BMW was faster. She knew that she was about to have him on the next corner.

The BMW took another sharp right, with its back end drifting and tires screeching and smoking, just as Nicolai attempted to run across the street. He tried to run around the car, but the still-moving back of the BMW knocked him off his feet. Hard. He fell to the ground, and rolled in agony. Jim caught up with them just as Catalina was getting out of the car. She popped open the trunk.

"Grab his feet!" she ordered Jim in a loud whisper. They shoved the injured Nicolai into the trunk and got back into the car. "I think he swallowed it," Catalina said to Jim calmly, and righted the BMW. She drove around until she found a garage. It was full of shiny expensive imports, with not a camera in sight. She pulled into an unlit area and parked.

"What are you doing?" asked Jim. Catalina gave him a look and pulled the Glock 19 out of her purse. She was pissed, and was no longer willing to play nice. From this point on this was her show, and Jim was just along for the ride. And he knew it. She dusted off the soles of her feet and slipped into her Louboutins before getting out of the car.

Catalina hiked up her dress to reveal a ceramic blade strapped to her inner thigh. Jim realized that she was prepared to cut Nicolai open if needed. She flipped the safety off her Glock and was about to put two bullets into Nicolai's chest as soon as she opened the trunk, but Jim stopped her.

"Just give me a minute," he requested. He was hoping that Catalina was wrong in thinking that Nicolai swallowed something in order to keep it safe. Jim patted him down and checked his hands. Nicolai's right hand was curled into a fist, a thin chain wrapped around his wrist. His hand was all scratched and bloody from being hit by the BMW. Catalina impatiently tapped her foot, and pretended to examine her manicure. Jim pried open Nicolai's stubby fingers, and there is was—a tubular object attached to the chain.

"I found it," said Jim. Catalina stopped tapping her foot. Jim shook the tube, something rattled inside.

"What is it?" she asked impatiently. "Does it open?"

"I don't know." Jim pulled on both ends. The tube came apart. He looked inside then shook out the contents into his palm. There was only one item—a micro SD card.

"Find his phone," suggested Catalina. Jim found the phone in Nicolai's back trouser pocket. It was a handmade luxury Vertu in jet alligator. Catalina plucked the phone out of Jim's hand and popped open one of the gullwing panels on the back. "Thirteen grand gets you an external card reader," she explained. Jim placed the SD card into her outstretched palm. Catalina plugged the card into the phone and flipped it over. "Let's hope he doesn't lock it," she said.

"Let me," asked Jim. Catalina handed him the phone. She watched him swipe on the screen with his thumb, his eyes narrowing in concentration. "I have it," he said suddenly.

"You unlocked it?" asked Catalina.

"No, I have *it*! It's what I've been looking for!" exclaimed Jim, without taking his eyes off the screen.

'We've been looking for! Remember who got you here,' Catalina retorted in her head. But all she said out loud was: "Oh. Good!" *Pop! Pop!* She shot Nicolai in the chest and shut the trunk closed. "Time to go!" she ordered Jim and got into the car. Jim just stood there, taken by surprise by her actions. Catalina nudged the car in reverse. Jim got her hint and hurried to get in. As she pulled out, she turned on the radio and flipped through the stations searching for something suitable to fit her mood. She finally found it –*Joyride* by The Killers. She smiled a little in satisfaction and turned up the volume. Jim was too engrossed in the images on the phone to notice the irony of her selection.

They found a place to dump the car, wiped clean of all possible prints, left Nicolai's dead body still in the trunk, and took the Metro back to Catalina's safe house. She sent a text to someone while still on the train. Back in the safe house, she asked Jim to clean up in the kitchen while she quickly changed. The square kitchen, with redwood cabinets and orange and yellow gingham wallpaper, had no dishwasher—Jim washed their orange polkadot dishes by hand. Catalina was ready to leave as soon as he finished. She tossed him a designer jacket to wear from the men's side of the vast wardrobe. They took all the luggage with them on the way out. After locking the door behind her, Catalina gently scratched on the neighbor's door and placed a large duffel bag on the floor. As they stepped out to the elevator banks, Jim noticed the neighbor's door open and a slim woman in a lace negligee pulled the duffel bag in without looking at the visitors. Jim gave Catalina a questioning look, but she mouthed that she would explain in the elevator.

"She's a prostitute. I leave her the clothes once I'm done with them. She's really good at keeping her mouth shut." Catalina left out the parts about the prostitute being a great source of all kinds of intel and for paying her to keep an eye on the safe house. The duffel bag, filled with everything Catalina wore tonight, was just a small and convenient token. Catalina kept the shoes, however.

They were picked up by the same Mercedes S-class that chauffeured them earlier. Catalina tossed a large envelope into the driver's lap when she got into the car. "I had to ditch the Bimmer," she explained. "This should cover it." The driver grunted but pocketed the cash.

45

They returned to the Ritz, pretending to be one happy drunk couple as they stumbled through the lobby. The driver was instructed to wait an hour, then come and pick them up. Catalina tossed everything she unpacked back into the suitcases they left in their room. She finished rather quickly and just plopped down on the large turned-down bed. She slowly sunk into the fluffy duvet and raised her arms over her head. Jim remained standing by the window, captivated by the dazzling view of the Red Square.

"How do you sleep at night?" he asked suddenly.

"With one eye open. You know that," she answered. "That's not what you're really asking, is it?"

"Nope," he said, gently twisting the sheer curtain between his fingers. "So how *do* you sleep at night?"

"Like a baby," she said calmly, and rolled over to her stomach so she could face him. "This curiosity, is it because I was about to gut that poor sap for a little flash drive?"

"Something like that."

"There is a difference between you and me, between how we were trained. You kill for God and Country, your actions save lives and make a world a better place. Or at least that's what you've been told," she smiled a little. "You went through psych evals, drills, God knows what else… just to see if you can stomach taking a life. You pull that trigger because at the end of that barrel there is a threat. Me… I do it for money. Lots and lots of money."

"So you don't care about your target?"

"No, not anymore. I used to be curious about why someone wanted someone else dead, but curiosity is a dangerous thing. It can kill you." She sat up on the bed, crossing her long legs. Jim realized that she was hinting at Dr. Wilson, the London job that put her on Jim's radar in the first place. The reason she took that job was because she discovered that Wilson was abusing his wife, and she nearly paid for that curiosity with her own life.

"How old were you when you did your first job?" He prodded again.

"I'm not answering that one."

"Why not?"

"Call it self-preservation," she answered. "But I was a lot younger than you. Anything else?"

"Biggest payday, how much?" he threw at her. "Don't worry, off the record."

"Ha, off the record? I'll hold you to that one... Chen. Before him, Africa was my biggest contract. It got even bigger because of all the extra bodies... Thanks by the way! I probably owe you a commission, but they did not pay in currency."

"What did they pay with?" he decided to let the remark about extra bodies slide, even though she was talking about killing his team.

"Real estate. On Embassy Row in DC. Only it's not there anymore," she said with a wink.

"Wait, what? That was *your* house? You lived there?" He walked away from the window and sat down on one of two apple-green brocade benches by the foot of the bed.

"You're just finding that out? I should've kept it then."

"Man, we totally missed that one. I knew there was a connection, but I thought it was because the Africans still owned it. No wonder they did not raise a big fuss over the explosion and demanded that they handle the investigation instead of the FBI… Man, totally missed that!"

"Don't beat yourself over it, it wasn't a message or anything like that," said Catalina with a mischievous smile.

"Why did you blow it up then?"

"I think you guys call it *protocol*. I was supposed to be dead, remember? So, my *'protocol',*" she made air quotes with her hands, "was that my non-Sicilian residence goes up in smoke. In case the authorities ever find out where I lived, there is nothing left to investigate."

"So you won't ever have to blow up your villa? Is that because no one on the island is dumb enough to go dig into your personal life?"

"Something like that," she said and smiled again. Catalina's phone, laying face down on the duvet next to her, vibrated. "Car's here, time to go."

The Gulfstream was already on the tarmac when they pulled up. Fernando rushed out of the plane and quietly exchanged a few urgent words with Catalina in Sicilian. She frowned and hurried into the plane. Jim followed close behind. A couple of minutes later they were closing the doors with the pilot announcing that they were cleared for take-off. The air filled with a sense of urgency, and Jim's insides started to constrict with worry. Something was off. Fernando handed Catalina a folded piece of paper and went to handle their luggage. Catalina read the paper, then uttered some pretty colorful Italian words and tossed the paper into Jim's lap. Jim picked up the paper and looked at the contents. It was a handwritten note:

Sat call from Don Carlo. Bulanovs are not Russian. Chechen mob.

Suggested you abort.

"Shit!" was the only thing that came to Jim's mind at this point. "When did he call? You're just getting this? Shit!"

"Butler didn't know where we were, I didn't give him the details! He checked with the driver but we were already in play. And, if you knew they were Chechen mob, would it change anything?"

"I probably wouldn't hit their precious son with a car and then leave him dead in the trunk! I doubt they'll take that lightly." Jim searched for his seatbelt as the plane accelerated.

"Oh yeah, we would have just politely asked Nicolai to hand us the SD card… It's done. *Finito*." Catalina leaned back in her seat and shut her eyes. She was tired, and at 30,000 feet all she wanted was some peace and quiet. There was nothing she could do about the Chechens so why worry about it at this moment? 'Deal with one problem at a time,' Nonno always said to her. Catalina could sense Jim was not happy with her answer. Fernando, able to read Catalina's body language, dimmed the cabin lights and came over to cover Catalina with a cashmere plaid blanket. It was a statement to Jim that there would be no conversations on this flight. He got the message and left her alone.

46

Provincia di Palermo, Sicily

As soon as the plane landed, Catalina took off to see Don Carlo and Luciano. Jim was escorted back to her villa. She was gone for a long time, so Jim swam laps around the pool to occupy himself. When Catalina returned, she sat down at the edge of the pool, putting her feet into the water. Jim swam up to her.

"What's up?" he treaded water next to her, not ready to get out yet.

"Nothing. What's your next move?" she asked.

"I went through the card during our flight. Peel didn't copy the files. He just pulled everything up on his computer, then took pictures of the screen. You can see parts of his office in the corners."

"Well, that's one way to avoid your security protocols, I guess."

"Yep, he's one sneaky son of a bitch."

"So what do you want to do?" Catalina had her sunglasses on and Jim could not read her face. He had a feeling there was a reason to her questions.

"Well, it would be nice to have a small conversation with him. For starters."

"Then how do we flush him out? He'll have to come across the pond, I'm not going back stateside."

"Easy. McCarthy can bring him over." Jim finally pulled himself out of the pool and sat down next to her. Fernando appeared out of nowhere to silently hand him a towel.

"McCarthy? How?" asked Catalina with curiosity in her voice.

"I'm MIA, remember?" Jim wrapped himself up in the fluffy, and warm, towel. "I surface, my trusty sidekick runs to my side, Peel won't be able to resist and follow. We just have to tell McCarthy to leave some breadcrumbs, to make it foolproof."

"With Peel's shoddy tradecraft, they'd have to be the size of a sourdough loaf for him to notice! How are you going to surface?"

"You're gonna have to let me use a phone. I need to make a call," said Jim, and looked Catalina straight in the face. She slid the sunglasses down her nose and gave him a look.

Catalina's response to Jim's request for a phone call was rather blown out of proportion, Jim thought. He would have been fine using a burner cell, but instead she turned it into an elaborate adventure. Jim thought it was overkill, Catalina called it 'self-preservation.' Late afternoon, she took him out on her boat—a gorgeous Aquariva Super runabout—several miles offshore and away from Bagheria. The Aquariva Super, named *Sophia* after Don Carlo's favorite Italian actress, was a stark contrast to the Donzi 43ZR she blew up in Miami. *Sophia* had soft classic lines with a timber deck and elegant leather on the steering wheel. She was also a lot slower. Catalina told Jim that at first she wanted to get another Donzi, but Don Carlo insisted she choose something more classic in design. 'More mature,' were the exact words he used.

Once Catalina reached a spot she was satisfied with, she handed Jim a Virtu phone, one very similar to Nicolai's. This one was in navy leather.

"Their network's encrypted, your call will be secure.

And if your friends GPS you, at least you're nowhere near our homes. We can live with that," she explained to Jim when he raised an eyebrow in question.

"And what are you going to do? I was hoping for a bit of privacy." Jim was trying to quickly figure out how to say what he needed without Catalina figuring it out.

"Oh, don't you worry," she responded. She took off her silk long dress with kimono sleeves, revealing a tiny black bikini, then reached into her bag for a pair of head-phones. The headphones were a large elaborate crown-like Dolce&Gabanna creation of gold, red leather and Swarovski crystals.

"What?" she asked Jim when she noticed him sup-pressing a comment on the over-the-top headphones. "They're a Christmas gift from the Triplets."

"The Triplets?" inquired Jim.

"My aunts. They're not really Triplets, I just call them that." She plugged the red headphones into her phone and went aft to sunbathe on the tanning deck.

Jim watched her stretch herself out on a large white leather cushion. For a moment the urge to join her washed over him, but he willed himself to turn his back. He took a deep breath and dialed a long distance number. The call was answered after first ring. "Code in please," said an unemotional female voice on the other end. Jim exhaled and identified himself.

———

New York, SAD

McCarthy sat down at his desk, confused. He was try-ing to figure out what was Campbell thinking, calling in like that. McCarthy had just finished having a conversa-tion with Peel, who announced that he was just informed that Campbell wanted to come in from the cold. Peel asked McCarthy if he knew that his friend was alive, McCarthy said no. Peel did not believe him, but did not say anything. He told McCarthy that he was assigned with bringing Campbell in, and that as soon as he had the operation plan he would share it with McCarthy since of course he must be eager to see his friend return to the US as soon as possible. McCarthy could feel Peel's eyes follow his every move as he returned to his desk. And so he just sat and stared at his computer, trying to figure out what was in Campbell's head. He did not expect him to return, he expected him to stay with the Benedettos. McCarthy himself was looking for a quiet way out of the Company business. 'What on earth are you doing?' McCarthy asked Campbell in his head. 'You could have gotten Peel without coming in. I could've done it for you!' His Company-issued cell phone rang. He looked at the caller ID, it said 'unknown caller'. He peeked at Peel's office over his cubicle wall before answering.

"Hey buddy." McCarthy heard Campbell's voice.

"What the fuck are you doing?" asked McCarthy without a warm welcome.

"And hello to you too!" said Campbell. "I need you to meet me in Frankfurt. Make sure you bring the package."

"The package…" McCarthy was confused. And then it dawned on him. "Oh! Got it! When?"

"The sooner the better. I'll meet you at the usual location."

"Done. See you soon." McCarthy hung up. He peeked over his cubicle wall again, this time just for show. Then he pulled up commercial flights to Frankfurt from JFK. He was looking for one with plenty of seats still available, since he was not coming alone. One flight looked promising, two days from now. He booked it right then and there, knowing that the transaction was going to be noted. Just to make sure, he used his personal credit card as well in order to establish as much of a trail as possible, yet still look somewhat discreet. He could sense Peel's eyes on the top of his head. McCarthy scribbled 'FRA' and the date of his flight on a pad of paper. He got up from his desk, ripped off the paper he just scribbled on, folded it up and slipped it into his coat pocket. Then he gathered his things and left.

Peel watched McCarthy from his office. He noticed that McCarthy took a call on his cell, then watched him do something on his computer before leaving the office. Peel picked up his phone and dialed a number.

"Yeah, I need to pull the last call on McCarthy's phone," he said to someone on the other line. "Encrypted line? What? Well, can you at least get a location?" he checked to see if McCarthy returned to his cubicle as he waited for an answer. "Somewhere in the Mediterranean. That's all you got. You guys are useless!" and he hung up. 'Somewhere in the Mediterranean…' he thought. Campbell was traced to the same general area. The call McCarthy got must have come from Campbell. 'Those two are awfully close,' he said to himself. Peel left his office and slowly strolled over to McCarthy's desk. There was a blank pad of paper on top of some files. Peel picked up the pad and looked it over. He could see indentations on the top sheet. He grabbed a pencil out of a ceramic mug with MIAMI emblazoned on it and rubbed the lead over the sheet. The rubbing revealed a couple of letter shapes and possibly numbers. Peel could make out F-R-A. 'France?' he asked himself. He noticed that McCarthy forgot to log out of his computer before he left. It was a breach of protocol, but instead of logging McCarthy off Peel seized the opportunity to snoop around the man's computer. He checked McCarthy's browser history and found a search for international flights out of JFK. FRA was the airport code for Frankfurt, Germany. McCarthy must be meeting Campbell in Europe. Peel looked at the numbers on the paper he clutched in his hand, they corresponded to a date. He hurried back to his office to get himself on the same flight.

When Nick got home, well before lunch, Marina was waiting for him with a printout of full instructions from Sicily. She picked them up from Mark just an hour before. Nick read and reread them carefully, committing every detail to memory before burning the printout. That night Marina and Nick moved to a safe house lined up by Marina's mob connections. Nick was not sure yet what he was going to do after he hooked up with Campbell in Frankfurt, but he knew he was not returning to the CIA. He spent the next two days, before his flight to Germany, developing several exit strategies. He was surprised how easily Marina agreed to walk away from her business she worked so hard on building and follow him into the unknown. "The business is just a front anyway," she told him, "my friends put it together for me, and they can do whatever they want with it. I can reinvent myself somewhere else."

47

New York

Not wanting to leave anything to chance, McCarthy spent the night before his flight back in the loft above Marina's business. He let Peel tail him there from the office, then watched discretely from the window as Peel paced up and down across the street for hours.

Marina arrived to keep him company. For the first time ever, she brought Chinese takeout. She brought eggrolls, potstickers, crab rangoons, and three different kinds of fried rice. They ate in the living room by the couch. Marina kicked off her heels and sat cross-legged on the rug in front of the coffee table. Nick stretched out next to her.

"So I went to check on Jim's place, and noticed two suits sitting in an unmarked car right across from his building. I hightailed it out of there as fast as possible," she brought up to Nick between mouthfuls of fried rice.

"Must be the Feds. I'm sure whomever Campbell called filed all the right paperwork. They'll be sitting on his place from now on," explained Nick before taking another pork potsticker. "Kudos for noticing them."

"My Daddy taught me how to pick them out at a very early age," sassed Marina.

"Smart man. Would love to meet him one day," said Nick, meaning every word.

"He's got a nickel left. Then you can meet him." Marina reverted to her seasoned New Jersey mob lingo now that she no longer needed to keep up appearances with

Nick. He found it refreshing and utterly hilarious.

"Can you help me pack after we're finished?" he asked.

"Sure. Can you bring a piece with you or no?"

"No. I'll just pick one up once I get there."

"Be careful then. And if anything, use a belt. It's messy, but effective," advised Marina.

"A belt? What for?"

"You know," she made a noose gesture around her neck, stuck her tongue out and pretended to die.

"Oh… for that!" Nick got her point. "I better wear one of good pliable leather then."

"Take the Italian one I gifted you for Christmas, it's perfect!"

"I wonder why…" teased Nick. Marina gently punched him in the arm.

Nick peeked out the window before going to bed, Peel was gone. Nick went to bed relieved that no one was watching his every move.

McCarthy arrived at the John F. Kennedy International Airport early and breezed through the security check by flashing his official cover government ID. He picked up a *New York Times* and a *Maxim* at a newsstand and carefully navigated through throngs of travelers. There was a small bar across from his departure gate and McCarthy rolled his little carry-on suitcase up to the counter and settled in with a pint of Guinness and a ham and cheese sandwich.

He had a good vantage point from his little perch—he could see the entire waiting area for his gate, along with a partial view of the next one. There was a huge sea of over-stuffed luggage in front of the gate next to his. He noticed a lot of Apple laptop boxes tightly secured to suitcases. The passengers slowly circled around the enormous pile, like dogs on patrol, keeping a close eye on their bags and Apple boxes. McCarthy had never seen anything like it.

'Where is this all going?' he wondered. He craned his neck to check out the flight destination. Moscow. 'Oh my God, they came here to shop!' he realized. He wondered if any of the Russian tourists visited a museum, or at least the Statue of Liberty. 'We should just let them all in during Black Friday—they'll solve our deficit problem in one day,' he thought with a chuckle. He ordered another pint and checked his phone for any messages. There was only one, from Marina, wishing him a safe and pleasant flight.

It was another hour before Peel showed up. Unlike McCarthy, he did not use his government ID, and had to endure a long security line along with a patdown just because he huffed and puffed when he was asked to remove his shoes. Peel circled the waiting area in front of their gate several times before noticing McCarthy by the bar. He walked slowly by a couple of times, trying to appear casual. McCarthy pretended to be engrossed in his *Maxim*. Satisfied that McCarthy was present and did not notice him, Peel went in search of a bathroom.

McCarthy booked himself a business class ticket. Peel got coach, the last row by the tail. When the boarding started, McCarthy got in line. Peel held back, hiding behind a large German man. As McCarthy stepped on to the jetway, Peel suddenly cut in front of an old lady to get on the plane two people behind McCarthy. He followed him to the plane, and turned green with envy as McCarthy seated himself in a business class window seat. Peel proceeded all the way to the tail, grazing the already seated passengers with his shoulder computer bag as he went.

McCarthy got comfortable in his nice roomy seat with his reading materials and his iPad. The night before, Marina uploaded all the seasons of *The West Wing* for him so he had something to watch in case he suddenly found himself faced with a lot of downtime. McCarthy flagged down a flight attendant, quietly flashed his cover ID and asked if a certain passenger in the back of the plane was still in his seat. When she returned with a confirmation, he got out his phone to send one last text before takeoff.

<Package acquired> he sent to a number Campbell provided in his instructions.

<See you on the other side> was the reply.

48

Frankfurt, Germany

Peel just cleared customs and merged into the crowd of travelers, when something sharp stabbed him in his behind. He was then grabbed tightly by the arm and pulled to the side. His legs buckled under him and he felt dizzy. Another pair of hands pushed him into a wheelchair that suddenly materialized behind him. He lost all muscle control and was about to pass out.

"Herzlich willkomen bei Frankfurt, Herr Peel!" whispered a female voice into his ear with menace. He lost consciousness.

Peel sharply came to when a bucket of ice water was dumped on his head. He could not move, and he discovered that he was duct-taped tightly to the wheelchair. His body ached all over, his legs felt heavy and big, and he had a splitting headache. He was also now wet and cold. Peel carefully tried to move his head to look around, only to get slapped hard in the face. His head was grabbed by the chin and yanked back. The fingers were thin and cool, sharp nails dug into his skin. A bright light shone into his eyes, blinding him. He squinted and tried to turn away, only for the nails to dig harder into his face to hold him in place.

"He's good, you can have a little chat," said a female voice. His face was released. He heard heels clicking away.

"You're not staying?" inquired a male voice from somewhere behind Peel.

"No, but keep the door open. I'll make us a snack," said

the female. Peel's vision was still clouded by bright white dots swimming in wild circles, but he was able to make out a tall slim dark shape walking away. Another, a much wider and distinctly male, shape appeared in front of him. Peel blinked rapidly to try to regain his vision. When his eyes finally focused, and he saw the man standing in front of him, a wave of nausea suddenly hit him. Campbell.

Catalina busied herself in the kitchen, keeping one eye on the activities in the next room. Unlike her father who liked to just beat the information out of someone—Frank called it 'old school'—Campbell preferred chemical assistance. Just like her. She started on making a pile of sandwiches and turned on the kettle, anticipating Campbell's need for a cup of Earl Grey.

The conversation did not last long, it was less than five minutes later when Jim stomped into the kitchen.

"Hmm, not in a talkative mood, is he?" Catalina asked calmly.

"Nope."

"Ok, plan B." She wiped her hands on a kitchen towel, grabbed a little black pouch off the counter and headed into the other room.

Jim made himself a cup of Earl Grey tea, grabbed a sandwich, and sat down at the kitchen table to watch.

Catalina wore a denim shirtdress—resembling a large man's buttondown shirt she just picked up off the bedroom floor—loosely belted around her waist, and a pair of teal and white stiletto Louboutin sandals with overlapping orange elastic straps. He knew she was packing, yet he had no idea where she was hiding it. Catalina stopped in front of Peel, slowly pulled closer the chair that Jim was sitting in a moment ago, put her long and tan stilettoed leg up on the chair, and started looking through the little black pouch. She finally produced a vile and a syringe. Peel snorted—an attempt to put on a brave face.

"You know," responded Catalina in a calm and even tone, "you pissed all over the trunk. Now the car reeks and I'll have to get another one." The mentioning of Peel peeing himself wiped the smirk off his face, exactly what Catalina intended. "You're nothing but a pest. Lucky for you, I'm really good at pest control."

Peel, his head still hurting, forced himself to look up in order to see the woman's face. She was stunningly beautiful, yet when she cocked her head a little to the side and looked at him with her steel-blue eyes—the hair on the back of his neck rose and chills ran down his spine. Unlike Campbell's eyes, full of rage and vengeance, her eyes were full of nothing but cold and calculated menace.

"I'm not sure if the needle's clean," she continued, examining the syringe. "So if you pick up a nasty viral disease, I apologize." She slowly filled the syringe with contents of the vile, then grabbed him by the face. He squirmed, trying to free from her grasp, but she simply tightened her grip. Catalina yanked his head to the side, exposing his neck, and plunged the needle all the way in. Peel felt burning liquid spread from his neck down. The feeling was uncomfortable. His heart rate increased rapidly, he began to pant slightly. Catalina watched his pupils dilate before letting go of his head. She lowered her leg off the chair, took her little black pouch, and returned to the kitchen.

"I'd say we give it half an hour, just for good measure. Let him suffer for a while," she commented, dropping the empty vile into the kitchen trash. The syringe was disposed of into an empty water bottle. Jim cocked an eyebrow in question. "What? No need for some poor garbage man to get stabbed accidently by a used needle," she explained, tossing the closed bottle into the trash.

"Safety first!" agreed Jim with a smile. "Sandwich?"

49

It was getting late. They were working Peel over for hours. He was talking, only half the time nothing made any sense. He was spinning tales for so long that even he could no longer tell the difference between his lies and reality. At some point, Catalina realized that Peel truly believed that he was superior and more intelligent than anyone else. He was still under the impression that he was going to walk out of this alive, and somehow turn it to his advantage. She was getting tired and wanted him dead. But he was not her kill, unless he forced her hand. And he was getting darn close.

Catalina changed into a pair of skinny jeans and a black boatneck tee with half sleeves. The towering stilettos were replaced with a pair of Chanel flats. She wore a leather holster with a Glock 19 under each arm, and twisted her long dark hair into a low bun. She wanted Peel to realize that the game was about to change.

"Can I talk to you for a sec?" Catalina asked Jim from the kitchen. He left Peel and came over.

"Why don't you two just go fuck?" Peel suddenly yelled and started to laugh uncontrollably. Jim continued into the kitchen, choosing not to respond. Catalina, however, had had enough. She stomped into Peel's room and pistol-whipped him to the side of his face with the butt of her Glock, knocking him unconscious.

"Enough!" she turned to Jim. "Kill him already! What are you waiting for? You've already got enough to write home about, how much more do you need? At this point, he's just making shit up!"

"I can't kill him. I have to deliver him," responded Jim quietly.

"Deliver him? To whom?"

"The Company. When I called in, I said I could flush out the traitor. They told me to bring him in."

"The Company? The same Company that left you to die in China? The same Company that employs this fucker?" she angrily pointed to Peel. Catalina was starting to fume. And she rarely lost control of her emotions. "It was me, who rescued you! Me, who killed Chen-the-Chin! Me, and my Family, who got you to Peel! And now I'm asking you to kill him. He's seen me, he knows our relationship. He's gonna serve it up to your Company assholes, and it's gonna be us who's going to go down. Don't you realize that?"

"If I bring him in, they turn a blind eye to us," Jim said, gesturing to her and then to himself. "That's the deal."

"Oh, please!" Catalina dramatically rolled her eyes. "Here," she pulled her Glock from her right side and handed it to Jim. "The only way to keep 'us' quiet is to shut him up. Go, deal with it!" she pointed toward slumped over Peel.

"No," Jim put the gun on the kitchen table. Catalina was about to grab it and pop Peel herself when she suddenly heard a faint chime coming from the small bedroom off the kitchen. Her satellite phone. The phone that was reserved for Family only. Only everyone knew she was working at the moment, she should not be getting calls. Ferruccio, who was positioned in a flat across the street to provide her with cover, was the designated point of contact. The only other time this phone rang was when Mark called one fateful night, asking for help. She killed his mother-in-law for him after that call. The phone chimed again. She was not imagining it, Jim heard it too. Catalina left the kitchen and went into the bedroom. She had just dug out the phone from a concealed compartment of her bag, when the burner in her back pocket vibrated. Text. Ferruccio.

<Answer the phone.> said the message. The satellite phone started to ring again. Catalina swiped right and brought the phone to her ear.

"*Pronto*," she answered.

Jim watched from the kitchen as her face suddenly drained of all color. She turned away from him. He was about to come to her, when she disconnected the call. Catalina walked over to the window and shut the blinds. Then, grabbing a jacket out of her bag, she walked over to the kitchen table and holstered the Glock she gave to Jim. She had a strange look on her face, but Jim could not read her.

"I need some fresh air," she told him.

"Everything OK?" he asked.

"Yes," she answered in an even and controlled tone. He did not believe her. "Kill him," she said suddenly, nodding toward Peel. "Oh I will." And she walked out the front door. Jim heard her heading down the stairs. He walked over to the closed bedroom blinds and cracked them open just enough to see the street. He watched as Catalina crossed the street and headed left. At the corner, a young man separated himself from a building and joined her. Jim recognized him—Ferruccio. At that moment it dawned on him that no matter what was going on between him and Catalina, the Family always came first.

Catalina returned hours later, and found the flat eerily quiet and surrounded by darkness. She drew her Glock, and slowly made her way into the bedroom. She found it empty. Across the street, back in his nest, Ferruccio had just turned on his night vision goggles when he caught Catalina's shape with a drawn weapon. He immediately assumed his position behind his sniper rifle, scanning Catalina's flat for signs of anyone else. He had to take several deep breaths to steady his jumping nerves, the shocking news from the Family during the last couple of hours severely shook him up.

Catalina went through the small bedroom, bathroom, and kitchen—all clear. There was no sign of anything wrong, yet Jim was nowhere and she had a really bad feeling in the pit of her stomach. She walked into the room where they kept Peel and discovered it was empty as well. The duct tape that held Peel in the wheelchair was cut. She stormed into the kitchen—the counter was covered in their dirty dishes. Catalina found the little black pouch, and emptied its contents onto the kitchen table. A vile of stimulant, designed to counteract the effects of the drugs so the victim could somewhat move, was gone. She realized with a sinking feeling, that while she was gone, Jim took the opportunity to steal away Peel. He was returning to the Company and using Peel as his entry card.

"Campbell! You son of a bitch!" exclaimed Catalina, suddenly swiping her arm across the kitchen counter in rage. The dishes crashed on the floor, shattering into hundreds of pieces, glass shards flying in every direction. Ferruccio grabbed his rifle and ran across the street.

———

Brooklyn Heights

Ari was sitting on the small couch in Mark's apartment, reading to Sofia, when a loud unfamiliar *beep beep* of a telephone suddenly filled the room. Mark stilled in front of his computers. Sofia tensed in Ari's arms. *Beep,*

beep! Mark got up and took large strides toward the kitchen sink. Ari stopped reading and watched in silence, with Sofia on his lap. *Beep, beep!* Mark opened the sink cabinet and searched for something deep inside it. To Ari's surprise, he pulled out something rectangular wrapped in plastic. *Beep, beep!* said the package. With shaky hands, Mark ripped the bag and unwrapped a black satellite phone. He unfolded the thick antenna just as the phone angrily beeped again. *"Pronto!"* was the only word Mark said. Ari watched as Mark's face registered shock, as he brought his shaky hand to cover his mouth, as his eyes filled with tears. All Mark managed was "ok" before the phone slipped out of his grasp. Ari put Sofia on the rug, and walked over to Mark. He gently guided him to the couch, then poured him a glass of cold water. Mark sat hunched over on the edge of the couch, eyes filled with tears. Ari sat next to him.

"My… He… I… My sister… I need my sister…" mumbled Mark. Ari picked up the satellite phone off the floor and handed it to him. "I can't… I shouldn't… She's on a job."

"Mark, dear, I think the job probably got canceled at the moment. Call her," gently said Ari, patting Mark on the hand for reassurance. Mark dialed Catalina's number.

"Mark?" answered Catalina on the first ring. Ari got up from the couch and scooped up Sophia from the floor. Together they went into the bedroom to give Mark some privacy.

"I… I just heard," managed Mark slowly.

"I know honey, I know. I told them to call you. I need you to get home. I'll see you at home," she said soothingly, yet Mark detected a strain in her voice. He knew his sister all too well, the strain was not from the bad news they all received.

"Where are you? Are you still with that guy?" asked

Mark. He did not want to say Campbell's name in front of Ari.

"That son of a bitch changed the game plan when I stepped out to take the call! I don't have time for this shit." Catalina explained through gritted teeth.

"Lina, leave it. Please. It can take forever, you don't have forever. You need to be home. Kill him another day." Mark pleaded.

"Nothing will happen for at least three days. Everyone needs to get over to Sicily, including you, and that'll take a while. Our Consigliere is handling things. I have three days. If I can't finish it in three days, I'll send the boys over to take care of it."

"I know he pissed you off, but can't you let this one go for now?" asked Mark.

"No loose ends, remember? He's my loose end. And I can't have any loose ends. Not anymore." Catalina said slowly, evenly. She waited for Mark to read between lines.

"Oh..." said Mark, suddenly understanding to what she was alluding. "I see... I'll see you in three days then. Good luck!"

"Thanks, bro. Mark, did you tell Ari yet?"

"No, why? They didn't know him."

"Tell Ari. And if they want to come with you, let them come."

"Ok, sis. I will," assured Mark. Catalina said her good-byes and hung up.

Mark tossed the phone on the couch, and went to the bedroom to talk to Ari. He found Ari setting up opened suitcases on the bed, ready to start packing up Mark and Sofia. 'The old man doesn't miss thing,' thought Mark lovingly. Sofia played with a stuffed animal inside one of the suitcases. Ari looked up at Mark, freed a little space on the bed and patted it as an invitation for Mark to sit down. He moved aside another suitcase and sat next to Mark.

"Talk." Ari ordered. Mark took a deep breath, tears suddenly filling his eyes again.

"He's dead. My…," he could not continue before losing it completely.

50

Hamburg, Germany

"Nervous?" Catalina asked Ferruccio. "Good. Nervous is good first time around. If you're not nervous, then you'll get cocky. And cocky gets you killed." She walked over to him and checked that his Kevlar vest was fastened properly.

Catalina and Ferruccio had been getting ready for the past couple of hours. They moved to Catalina's Sanctuary, hidden in the conveniently forgotten corner of a shipyard. The converted metal shipping container was designed for one person, the space was extremely tight with both of them. Yet, they managed just fine. Silence and efficiency in movement was key. They did not have to be stuck in the Sanctuary for long, Campbell was fast in setting up an extraction for Peel, afraid that Catalina would come after them.

They slept soundly—this Sanctuary came with comfortable bunk beds. They ate well—the Sanctuary was well stocked with gourmet canned goods. They carefully scouted the extraction location, set up their nest, and secured their exit routes. On the way back from their outings they stopped at a market to pick up fresh food and wine to complement their meals. They had several hours to relax, in silence, before packing up. Catalina took a nap, and suggested Ferruccio do the same. He attempted to do some reading, but then dozed off as well. When the gentle chime of the alarm clock woke them up, both were refreshed and full of energy.

Catalina carefully checked and loaded her weapons, keeping an eye on how Ferruccio loaded his. They helped each other getting into their custom-made Kevlar vests. Ferruccio's was brand new—this was going to be his first time out in the field. Catalina's vest was well worn. She patted it lovingly, like an old-time friend, when she put it on.

As they packed their gear, Catalina kept a watchful eye on a wall of screens—the tracking signal was holding. The red pulsating dot was dancing in place a little, but not making any major moves. She motioned to Ferruccio to transfer the tracking to his phone and shut down all the systems. He nodded. It was now his job to monitor their target. They spoke very little to each other in the last couple of days, exchanging only mission-critical information. The mood was focused, yet somber. They both knew that as soon as their operation was over, the reality of the situation back home would catch up and they would fall apart at the seams.

———

Campbell was pacing. He was dressed and ready to go. He knew he would calm down once he boarded the plane with Peel in one piece. The lack of action from Catalina was disturbing. At a minimum, he expected an angry phone call. Instead, all he got was silence, as if she just vanished. "Don't look at me! I don't have a clue!" McCarthy defensively answered more than once to Campbell's questions about Catalina's whereabouts. McCarthy himself was rather quiet and distant. If he disapproved of Campbell's actions, he did not say anything.

When Catalina abruptly left their Frankfurt safe house with Ferruccio in tow and did not yet return an hour later, it suddenly dawned on Campbell that he could move Peel and call for an extraction. It was a rash decision, he did not think all the way through possible consequences, nor did he consider his relationship with Catalina at that moment. He borrowed a car, and moved Peel to a cramped CIA safe house McCarthy was hanging out in. When McCarthy saw Peel—bound and gagged in the trunk of a stolen vehicle, yet alive—he was shocked. "I thought you were going to kill him," he commented with disappointment. "They want him alive," explained Campbell. 'Always the Company man,' thought McCarthy as he helped his friend to get Peel out of the trunk.

It took 48 hours for a Black Ops team to arrive and assist with the extraction. To be safe, Campbell demanded that the team be comprised of men that have never worked for Peel before. When the team arrived, neither Campbell nor McCarthy knew a single member. They were four large men with large guns, and they made the already cramped flat even tighter. They called themselves The Cavalry. They survived on pizza and beer, the stale smell of both quickly filled the air, and mixed with the overabundance of testosterone to produce an odor closely resembling a zoo. McCarthy missed the clean scent of Marina's Light Blue perfume. Sleeping was in shifts—Campbell wanted someone to guard Peel at all times. McCarthy felt small among these huge and seasoned men, even though he was not a short person himself. He retreated into the tasks Campbell assigned him and quietly watched from the sidelines as The Cavalry played with their weapons and argued with Campbell over airport strategies. A couple of times Campbell forgot McCarthy was even there. They were all in each other's way, and were still bumping into each other as they were gearing up to leave. One more day and they would most likely explode. It did not help that Peel kept calling everyone derogatory names and taunting Campbell and McCarthy every time his gag was removed.

"Do us all a favor and pop him!" said McCarthy to Campbell for the umpteenth time. "You're starting to sound like her," remarked Campbell. "Well, she does have a point," retorted McCarthy under his breath.

Finally, the team—Peel dressed in a bullet-proof vest— was ready to leave. McCarthy excused himself to the bathroom at the last moment. Campbell, knowing that the young man did not spend much time out in the field, did not think anything of it. Two black Suburbans waited for them on the street right in front of the building. 'Could we stand out even more?' thought McCarthy as he climbed into the same Suburban as Campbell and Peel. Campbell checked out the perimeter before getting into the car. Once inside, he checked his phone. Nothing. There was still no sign of Catalina. 'Whatever made her run out of the safe house must be far more important to her than this,' told Campbell to himself. One more hour and they'll be up in the air. A small wave of relief washed over him, relaxing his shoulders. McCarthy was starting to clench his jaw, however. He turned away from Campbell so his friend would not be able to read the tension on his face.

———

"No change in plans," Catalina informed Ferruccio after checking her phone.

"He's on the move," he responded.

"I hate this part," remarked Catalina after a while.

"What part?" asked Ferruccio.

"This. Waiting. I hate waiting for the target to arrive. Sometimes they even run late."

"Was there a time when the target did not even arrive?" asked Ferruccio curiously.

"Yeah. Politicians are the worst, they're always running late or changing their plans. Then you have to chase them all over again and set up somewhere else," said Catalina. Ferruccio detected a slight amusement in her voice.

"How dare they!" he joked. Catalina gave him a look with a raised eyebrow, but did not reprimand. This was the most conversation they had in days.

"What's the ETA?" she inquired.

"With traffic, about 45 minutes," responded Ferruccio. Catalina took a deep breath, then released it slowly. "Fine," she acquiesced.

51

Airbus Airport, Hamburg, Germany

The jet waited alone on the tarmac. The black Suburbans pulled up as close as possible to the roll-away stairs. The Cavalry disembarked, taking on defensive positions. There was not a cloud in the sky, the air was warm. Once in a while a small gust of wind would rustle the grass in the surrounding service fields and kick up the dust. There was not a person in sight, everyone had been pulled back. One of The Cavalry gestured an 'all clear' to Campbell and he got out of the car.

Campbell's phone rang just as he was reaching inside the vehicle to pull Peel out. The caller was unlisted, but he instantly knew who it was. Catalina.

"Last chance," she said as soon as he accepted the call. "You can do him right now and I'll get you out."

"No," Campbell answered. He halted and looked around. A gust of wind rustled his hair. All the buildings and rooftops in sight were cleared, security had been on full alert. The last sweep of the lone runway and the surrounding areas was finished right before they arrived. There was nowhere she could hide and he knew she was not capable of a long range shot. "No, I'm bringing him in," he said again. There was silence on the other end of the line. Then he heard her sigh.

"Very well. *Ciao!*" The line went dead.

Campbell leaned back into the Suburban and grabbed Peel's arm. His hands were zip-tied, he was moving slowly.

Campbell impatiently pulled him out. He did not notice that McCarthy was still inside the Suburban.

"Did your psycho girlfriend ask you to kill me?" Peel asked with a laugh. Campbell pushed him toward the plane without the answer. Peel looked around and smiled. "Clever boy," he said, "she can't do me herself. No place to shoot from. Good!" And he stepped toward the bright yellow rollaway stairs. Campbell slowed down to check the surroundings one more time.

His eyes scanned The Cavalry surrounding the plane, mentally ticking off a roster. Adams, Thompson, Dunn, Butler … Where's McCarthy? Campbell halted. He looked around, then turned toward the Suburban. He saw McCarthy's hand on the car door yet he was not getting out. An alarm went off in Campbell's head. The word *'shit!'* was still leaving Campbell's lips, as Peel's head suddenly exploded and he fell forward. Campbell spun toward him and froze when he saw Peel's brains splattered all over the bright yellow stairs. She had the shot.

———

"Confirmed," stated Ferruccio. Catalina closed her eyes. "Campbell?"

"Not today," she answered and put down her rifle.

They quickly wrapped up their equipment and slid down the mountain of gravel they used as their nest. They moved swiftly and quietly through the trees surrounding the small stone yard located close to the runway that no one even thought of checking because it was too far away, got into a car they left on side of the highway covered in fake bushes, and merged into traffic.

———

Campbell stood over the body staring as a pool of blood slowly formed under it, oblivious to the sudden explosion of panicked activity on the tarmac. The Cavalry scrambled for cover. Someone pulled him aside and shoved him into a vehicle. It was good ten minutes before he realized that the car was moving and he turned to look at the driver. McCarthy.

"I thought I had it all covered," Campbell said in bewilderment.

"Then you still don't know anything about her," answered McCarthy, driving away as fast as possible. Campbell did not respond, just stared out the window.

"So now what? You're working for her now?" Campbell suddenly asked with anger.

"I had a choice to make and I chose saving the life of my friend and a life with someone I deeply love. I don't expect you to understand," McCarthy answered quietly.

"You called her from the bathroom, back at the safe house, didn't you? You gave her all the intel."

"I did call her, but she already had the intel. I just told her we were running on time." McCarthy confirmed.

"Had the intel? How the fuck did she know my operation details?" snapped Campbell.

"They'll probably kill me for this, but you might want to have your leg X-rayed. You don't want to be running around saving the world with a Mob tracker in your body," explained McCarthy and nodded toward Campbell's left thigh with his head. Suddenly Campbell remembered Catalina stabbing him with a large injection pen in Hong Kong.

"Oh, Jesus Christ!" was the only thing that came to Campbell's mind. McCarthy could not help but smile a little.

"What are you going to do? The Cavalry is going to report that you stayed in the car. There is no way they are going to take the fall for this." Campbell asked after a while.

"I'm going to drop you off at a rendezvous point per protocol and disappear. I'll dump the car, you guys can retrieve it later. And the rest you'll never know," McCarthy said with sadness in his voice. He gripped the steering wheel tighter and concentrated on traffic. Campbell waited for him to add more, but McCarthy stayed silent.

52

Catalina boarded the waiting plane in haste, Ferruccio right on her heels. The plane's engines were already on, itching to take off.

"Go, go!" she yelled toward the cockpit. The plane started to taxi away while a crewmember was still pulling the door closed. Ferruccio went to the cockpit to find out how fast they could make it to Sicily. He knew Catalina was going to demand the answer any minute.

"We've got a good tailwind, Captain said they can shave off about 20 minutes for sure," he reported five minutes later. Catalina nodded without saying a word. She was sitting with a straight back, stone faced, still wearing her aviators even though the shades were drawn and the cabin lights dim. Ferruccio was about to retreat to his seat, when she spoke.

"Check with Luciano that he made the calls. And find out when my brother arrives," she ordered.

"*Sí, Signora!*" replied Ferruccio with a little bow of the head. He retrieved a satellite phone from his bag and walked aft to make his call.

Catalina sat—immobile, staring into nothing—for a while, then dug through her bag she dropped by her feet. She found a phone, it was a burner but she knew the number she needed by heart. She dialed. The line was picked up on the first ring.

"I didn't get to say goodbye," she said in Sicilian instead of hello.

"No one did, honey. No one," said the strained voice on the other end.

"I should've stayed home, instead of playing friends with benefits. I should've been there." continued Catalina, her voice shaking a little. Her eyes started to well up and she quickly wiped of a tear with her index finger.

"You did exactly what he wanted you to do. We live with no regrets, remember?" the voice assured her. "I'll see you when you land. There is a lot to discuss."

"Ok," she sighed, "see you soon." Catalina ended the call.

She reclined her seat and lifted one of the window shades. "I miss you already," she whispered, looking out at the fluffy white clouds beneath the plane.

———

McCarthy took Campbell to Planten un Blomen park in the inner-city of Hamburg. He dropped Campbell off at the entrance far away from the rendezvous point, he would have to walk across to the other side to reach it. It was a beautiful day and the park was filled with people strolling around and picnicking on the luscious grass.

Their goodbye was brief and awkward. They shook hands and wished each other good luck and to stay safe. As McCarthy got back into the car, Campbell called out to him.

"I gotta know, where was she? I thought we were thorough, there wasn't anywhere for her to hide," he asked. McCarthy took a long look at him but did not answer. Campbell waited.

"I guess you didn't learn anything from Miami. She's always steps ahead." McCarthy silently debated whether to answer Campbell's question. "Fine… Most likely the stone yard past the runway. You cleared out all the planes, giving her a clear view," he finally answered.

"The stone yard… But that would have been…" A look

of utter bewilderment settled on Campbell's face as he attempted to compute the distance in his head.

"Just over 2000 yards," volunteered McCarthy and started the engine. "You should've done what she asked."

53

Provincia di Palermo, Sicily

Small raindrops lazily hit the windshields of Mercedes Benz S-class armored sedans that made up an incredibly long funeral procession. Monsignor Alessandro Benedetto, in his funeral robes, was waiting by the family plot and impatiently looking up at the sky. Nobody was getting out of their cars—they were waiting for the immediate family to come out first.

Catalina watched from the backseat as the rain drops hit the windshield. She waited for the wipers to swipe the drops away, but the drops were too small and too infrequent to set off the sensor.

"So, are we having rain or not?" she asked Mark, who was sitting next to her.

"Luciano said that he overheard Nunzio complain about his knees," reported Mark. "So we're most likely having rain."

"Great. Just what we need—a soggy funeral," sneered Catalina. "You better tell Alessandro to speed it up then." She opened a compact to check her makeup. Mark looked out the window at his fidgety uncle. "I think he's one step ahead of you," he said to his sister.

"Well… I guess we better get on with it then," she said and closed her compact with a snap. Mark straightened his tie, and waited for Catalina to lower the black veil over her face, before signaling the driver that they were ready to finally get out of the car.

The driver held the door open for Mark and Catalina. Mark got out first. He smoothed his suit coat, then took Catalina's outstretched hand to help her out of the car. The moment she was out, others followed in leaving their vehicles. A large crowd of mourners, all in black, was quickly gathering. Catalina smoothed a wrinkle out of her pencil skirt with a gentle swipe of her hand. Mark offered his hand—she took it. He leaned in and whispered: "Ready?"

"No," she whispered back. "All these people… They're all here… Make sure Ferruccio's keeping a list, we need to know exactly who's here."

"Don't worry, he's got it all under control," Mark assured her. They were walking slowly toward Zio Alessandro.

Even in grief, Catalina and Mark were a striking sibling pair—dressed in black, backs straight, chins up, their movements elegant and composed. Catalina wore a large brimmed hat with a lace veil. She wanted to hide her face—afraid that her emotions would betray her. They quietly greeted Alessandro, then took their seats in the front row. Catalina sat down in the white folding chair just on the edge of the seat: knees together, back straight, hands folded over her small black clutch in her lap. Mark sat on her left. Zio Nunzio waddled over and carefully took the seat next to Mark. A faint buzzing sound cut through the air, but nobody looked up—they were all used to the Interpol surveillance drones buzzing around every time there was a Mafia funeral. Alessandro waited for everyone to settle down and looked over at Catalina to signal him to start. Mark leaned over and whispered in her ear: "Are you ready now?"

"No," she answered as she slightly raised her hand signaling Alessandro to start the service.

———

Paris, France

La Brasserie de l'Isle Saint-Louis—with its red and gold awnings, and rattan café chairs surrounding marble-top tables—was located at the tip of the Île Saint-Louis in front of Notre Dame and featured panoramic views of the Seine. He chose the table outside, among the hustle and bustle of the lunch crowd. A waiter in a black vest, a crisp white shirt with sleeves rolled up to the elbows, and a long white apron approached him to take his order. He went with sole meunière and a glass of Sancerre. Shortly after his food arrived, a man in an off-the-rack gray wool suit joined him. He carried a leather briefcase that he sat at the foot of the table. The waiter materialized in front of him to take his order. The man eyed the sole meunière with suspicion and ordered steak and beer instead.

"You really should try the sole, it's a classic," suggested Campbell, pointing to his fish with a fork.

"I'm more of a steak and potatoes guy," said the gray-suited spook. "Interesting spot for a conversation."

"I like the food," returned Campbell. He chose this place strategically, it was out in the open and full of phone-obsessed tourists and old locals that noticed everything. He was really hoping to be back in New York already, and was pissed off when the Company ordered him to Paris to wait for further instructions. "What do you want? Unless you brought me a first class ticket home," Campbell carefully slid a piece of sole on the fork with his knife and placed it into his mouth.

"No ticket. Uncle wants to set you up on your own," answered the spook in a low voice, leaning in. He clammed up when the waiter appeared with his slab of meat and a beer. The waiter read the tension in the air and quickly disappeared. "Based in Europe. As a NOC of course. But with full resources," said the spook. Campbell raised an eyebrow and stopped chewing. "Pick your own team, although we still don't know where McCarthy is. Any ideas?" continued the gray suit. He tried to see if Campbell flinched at the mention of McCarthy, but Campbell's face revealed nothing. The spook attacked his steak and started cutting it up rather clumsily. Campbell grimaced in disgust at the man's obvious lack of table manners.

"I have no clue where McCarthy is. Just let him go, I owe him that much," said Campbell, slowly twisting his fork in his left hand. His right slipped under the table, and found his gun hidden under his napkin on his lap. "My own unit, huh?" he asked suspiciously.

"Yep. We figured you work best on your own. You know how this works. It's all set-up. Just say 'yes'," the spook explained with his mouth full.

"And the Benedettos?" asked Campbell.

"Consider them an asset. Aren't they dealing with a family issue right now?" he continued before finally swallowing. "Let's wait and see. I'm sure when the dust settles you can bring them into the fold." The spook shoved another piece of steak into his mouth. "Skills like that are very useful. And, we've been very generous with our fees," he washed down his steak with a chug of beer. Campbell lost his appetite.

"Fine… Yes," said Campbell. 'Not that I really have a choice here, do I?' he thought to himself.

"All righty then!" answered the spook cheerfully and chugged the rest of his beer. He wiped his mouth with his napkin and tossed it right on the plate. Under the table, his foot pushed the briefcase toward Campbell. "Sayonara then! You don't mind picking up my tab, will ya?" he said getting up. Campbell just waved him off as he reached for his wine glass.

The waiter reappeared and asked if there was anything else. Campbell looked at his unfinished fish and sighed, then asked for a cognac. The waiter politely suggested that the sole should reheat for dinner if the gentleman wished to take it with him. Campbell simply nodded yes. Once the waiter left, he slipped his gun back under his shirt and leaned in his rattan chair. The cognac arrived and Campbell sipped it slowly, watching the tour boats go up and down the Seine, his mind on Benedetto's sudden family issue. He wondered how Catalina was doing. Finally, his cognac empty, he paid his tab and left with the briefcase. His waiter watched him leave, then discretely pulled a phone out of his apron and sent a quick text. To Sicily.

Epilogue

London, England

It was a typical gray and overcast London day. Peter and Alexander Bulanov arrived earlier that day by their private jet. The arrival did not go unnoticed by the half a million CCTV cameras scattered all over London. Their movements were followed from the airport to the front door of their West London mansion. They were summoned to London by Ekaterina, Peter's wife and Alexander's mother. Both men preferred to be somewhere else at the moment.

The opulent and over-the-top Louis XIV furnishings in the newly appointed drawing room reflected the oligarch lifestyle of the Bulanovs, yet did absolutely nothing to lighten the somber mood. The mother, Ekaterina, decked out in black Chanel head to toe, stood by the large window slowly steaming. Her once dark hair was bleached and elaborately coiffed, and her Botox-injected face barely moved. Yet no amount of bleach or Chanel could cover up the peasant upbringing and the lack of pedigree.

Her eldest son, Alexander, stood next to the fireplace, quietly watching his mother. He knew that he was not going to like what she was about to demand. His father Peter sat uncomfortably in a gilded chair, checking his watch, waiting for his wife to explain why she summoned him and Alexander to London. Ekaterina and Peter lived separate lives, Ekaterina preferring to live in London full-time in an enormous mansion Peter bought her for over

40 million and then spent another 200 million redecorating. Peter and Alexander both jetset around the world under pretext of business, but still called Moscow home. Peter tried really hard not to be in the same city as his wife for more than 24 hours. But the funeral of their youngest son Nicolai forced them to spend an entire week under one roof. The week ended rather badly. Peter checked his watch again, and started tapping his foot slightly. Alexander watched his mother.

"So, my dear husband, what are you going to do about punishing those responsible for the death of my Kolechka?" she finally said.

"Absolutely nothing," said Peter. "He was collateral damage. If you want to continue our way of life," he made a sweeping motion toward their opulent surroundings, "you have to pay." He got up and walked behind his gilded chair, back straight and chest out. 'Wrong answer, Pa!' thought Alexander. He looked at his mother—her face was slowly getting red and her nostrils flaring out. Not even Botox could hide her expression of rage.

"My son, my whole world, my reason for living, is 'collateral damage'? A price I have to pay?" she screamed, leaning forward and baring her teeth. Her massive Chanel pearls rattled. She stomped toward Peter and dramatically slapped him across the face. "You make them pay!" she screamed in his face, shaking her fists and stomping her foot. "Or I will tell everyone who we really are! Then we'll see about collateral damage!" She turned on her heel and stormed out of the room, slamming the massive English oak door behind her.

"Pa," called out Alexander to his father, who was rubbing his slapped cheek. "Pa!"

"*Shto!*" Peter finally reacted.

"Are you just going to stand there and take this shit?

She's nuts! She'll ruin everything!" pointed out Alexander angrily to Peter. "Moi Kolechka, moi Kolechka!" whined Alexander in a falsetto voice, mimicking his mother. "Mama's boy," he continued, grimacing in disgust. "She should blame herself for his demise, she raised a total moron!"

"That's enough!" suddenly boomed Peter. "Show some respect!"

"We'll expose ourselves… Our plans… Everything we worked for… There is so much at stake… Pa, you know this," pleaded Alexander, knowing that his words were falling on deaf ears. Peter would never be able to bring himself to kill his wife, and she knew just enough not to be ignored. Peter walked over to the window and looked out on his fabulous, even on such an overcast day, view of London. He could see his silver Rolls Royce Phantom parked on the street below, uniformed driver waiting. He looked down at his manicured hands, his enormous gold and diamond Rolex watch. He checked the time—one of his mistresses had tickets to the London Symphony Orchestra tonight. He looked out the window again. Far in the distance, dark stormy clouds started to form. 'Can't touch the American, we might need them. But the other one… It's just some Sicilian bitch, how hard could this be?' he thought. 'We didn't find anything on her, she's nothing, a nobody.' He looked at the forming storm clouds on the horizon, then drew the heavy curtains with a snap. He slowly turned to Alexander, decision made.

"Alexander… that Sicilian… kill her," he ordered.

About the Author

Katherine Brankin grew up on Leo Tolstoy and Fyodor Dostoevsky, but matured on Ian Fleming. Already being an accomplished designer and blogger of Driving Master Danny, writing fiction became just one more outlet for her imagination. The characters and their incredible stories just appeared in front of her one day and she took a chance.

Katherine lives in the suburbs of Chicago with her family and two nocturnal pets that keep her company when she writes at odd hours of the night fueled by large quantities of hot tea and antipasto platters.

For all things Catalina, visit www.whoiscatalina.com.

THE FAMILY GIRL

The Bennett Trilogy Book I

Prologue

Arlington, Virginia

To passersby they looked like a father and son enjoying the afternoon sun in the park. But that was not the case. This was their first and last meeting, and both were hoping that their paths would not cross again.

"Look, I was told that you could do this sort of thing… All I want is his research, which was mine to begin with… I made this guy, I pulled him out of that foul hole he worked in and gave him everything. And this is how he repays me? By refusing to give me the final product! That son of a bitch!… I really don't care how you do it, just get me my research. Or make sure that no one else gets it," the young man said to the old one between puffs of his cigarette.

"And you can't do it in-house?"

"Unfortunately for us, the S.O.B. is an American."

"You better be prepared to offer me something other than money for this. I've got money," the old man replied and readjusted the baseball hat he was wearing. He must have not been used to wearing one, for it seemed to bother him and he kept fiddling with it throughout their conversation.

"Full immunity. Past, present, future. You'll be untouchable. It's an offer you can't refuse," the young man replied after a minute and flicked his cigarette on the ground. It landed a couple of feet in front of them and lay there, slowly smoldering.

"Quoting *The Godfather* will not make me take your offer, nor does it make you a man," the old man answered and readjusted his baseball hat again. He sat deeper into the bench and sighed.

"Listen, I'll give you time to think about it. 24 hours. But you'd be foolish not to take me up on it," the young man finally said and got up to leave. "24 hours, after that the offer's off the table," and he walked away.

Late that night, an old man with a limp walked into a crowed pub and elbowed his way through the crowd to the phone in the back hallway by the bathrooms. He dialed a number and waited as it rang on the other end. The phone was picked up after one ring. The old man smiled.

"Consider it done. Send me the dossier," he said before anyone on the other line could say hello and hung up. He then pushed his way to the bar and asked for a double gin on the rocks. When the drink arrived, he lifted the glass a little in a small toast to himself and took a long sip. A big, satisfying smile spread on his face once the gin warmed its way down the pit of his stomach. Yet, to the bartender, who happened to witness this smile, the old man looked even more menacing than before. The bartender shuddered and moved to the other end of the bar, hoping for the man to leave.

1

January, present time

The ringing startled her at first. Then, an eerie feeling crept over her as she recognized the sounds. It was her satellite phone, given to her by her father to be used for family emergencies only. From anywhere in the world they could reach each other, untraceable.

She scrambled to find the phone, and finally got it on the last ring. "Yes?"

"Lina, it's me. I'm sorry. I should've listened to you…"

She listened without interruption while her older brother talked. By the end, he was sobbing. She stood in the middle of her bedroom clutching the phone, not reacting. Finally she managed to grind out through her clenched teeth: "I'll take care of it."

Evanston, Illinois

"Your daughter has a visitor Mr. Bennett," said the duty nurse at the NICU station. Mark's pulse stilled. This statement could not mean anything but more bad news.

"Who is it?"

"A woman. Your sister? She said she's in between business flights and only has a couple of hours for a visit."

Mark's heart started to beat again. Slowly. Uncertainly. He hadn't talked to or seen his sister since he defied the family and married. Yesterday was the first time they've spoken since that day. A day he came to regret for the rest of his life.

He walked down the corridor to the room where his newborn daughter was fighting to survive along with other preemies. Through the glass door, he could see a fur-clad woman standing next to her crib. 'And the devil does wear Prada,' he thought. The hydraulic doors opened silently as he approached. The woman turned her head.

"You have a beautiful baby," she said.

"What are you doing here? Why didn't you call?"

"I had to meet her, Mark," Catalina walked over to her brother. They stood there, in the door jam, silent, awkward, each looking each other over. She reminded him of their father with the same cold steel blue eyes. So cold was the look that he felt shivers down his back. She thought that he looked haunted. 'No shit, after living with those bitches, you'd be haunted too,' she smirked to herself.

"My mother-in-law had a heart attack, Lina," Mark finally whispered.

"Things happen. I'm sorry for your loss. Both of them," she replied. And with those words Catalina leaned over and embraced her brother.

"It's done. The will, everything. Daddy's on his way to help with the follow through. Don't fuck this up and you'll finally be free. That bitch should've driven into a tree a long time ago," she whispered into his ear. "All you have to do now is take care of your daughter and listen to the Family." She released him. "I'm going to miss my flight. I won't be able to make the funeral. Neither, at this point," she said out loud, mostly for the benefit of nurses buzzing in and out of the room.

She turned around to look at the sleeping baby one more time, then started walking out the door. At the door she paused and turned to Mark. "Girl's a Bennett, she'll make it. Say Hi to Daddy for me." And with that she was gone.

Mark just stood in the NICU room for a long time, silent, motionless. In his head he was reliving the last year. His late wife turned out to be a mean jealous woman who, out of fear that he'd finally leave her, tricked him into getting her pregnant. She was also a reckless driver who had so many accidents that her license was revoked. And yet she still drove herself even though her rich mother provided her with a car and a driver. Last week, while being 30 weeks pregnant, she plowed into a tree. She died in the hospital, on the operating table, as her child was being delivered. Mark had to make a choice: save the baby or her. He chose the baby. Which meant that his mother-in-law lost her only child. The apple didn't fall far from the tree in that family, as Mark's mother-in-law was truly a monster. Enraged over loosing her only child, she proceeded to immediately seek custody of the baby even though she didn't want her. She just wanted to hurt Mark. Desperate to keep his child, he broke down and called his sister. Deep down, he knew what he was truly asking her to do when he asked for her help.

He finally walked over to his baby's incubator and put his hand through. As he was stroking the baby's head he noticed a clock on the wall. His hand froze, and he shuddered. Sometime in the last twelve hours, his younger sister assassinated his mother-in-law. And he ordered the hit.

www.ingramcontent.com/pod-product-compliance
Lightning Source LLC
Chambersburg PA
CBHW021007120726
47905CB00009B/2901